"I didn't do it." Her words were muffled by his shirt.

"You don't have to say that to me."

Abigail looked up, her face streaked with tears and her eyelids red. "Thank you. You don't know what it means to have someone who believes in my innocence."

Her lips were close. So temptingly close that her breath brushed his lips when she spoke. Without thinking, he kissed her. Gently, Griffin's mouth met hers. Taking all the time in the world, he softly explored the delicate curve of her lips. As she tilted her head to one side, he caressed the seam of her mouth with his tongue.

Winding her arms around his neck, she lightly nudged his tongue with her own. And passion ignited in an instant.

Dear Reader,

There's nothing like a Coltons story to bring a smile to our lips and get our hearts racing. And the Coltons of Grand Rapids certainly live up to our expectations! As always, it's been a pleasure to be part of the team of amazing authors who bring these characters and their stories to life.

Having been through the foster care and adoption system himself as a young child, Griffin Colton is always the first to step up and help a child in need. But when that child is fostered by Abigail Matthews, the daughter of the man his family is investigating as part of one of the worst scams in Grand Rapids history, he knows he should back off. Things are complicated even further by the attraction he feels toward the beautiful research scientist.

Abigail's life is in turmoil. Her father is on the run and her own part in his dodgy dealings is in question. Now she is accused of malpractice and is suspected of murder. As her reputation sinks almost beyond repair, the only person who can help her is the very man she should avoid. Griffin is a Colton and his family has every reason to be suspicious of her. Yet she feels safe with him...

I'd love to find out what you think of Griffin and Abigail's story. You can contact me at:

Website: www.JaneGodmanAuthor.com

Twitter: @JaneGodman

Facebook: Jane Godman Author

Happy reading,

Jane

COLTON 911: SUSPECT UNDER SIEGE

Jane Godman

HARLEQUIN

ROMANTIC
SUSPENSE

Special thanks and acknowledgment are given to Jane Godman for her contribution to the Colton 911: Grand Rapids miniseries

Recycling programs
for this product may
not exist in your area.

ISBN-13: 978-1-335-62664-6

Colton 911: Suspect Under Siege

Copyright © 2020 by Harlequin Books S.A.

This edition published by arrangement with Harlequin Books S.A.

For questions and comments about the quality of this book, please contact us at CustomerService@Harlequin.com.

Harlequin Enterprises ULC
22 Adelaide St. West, 40th Floor
Toronto, Ontario M5H 4E3, Canada
www.Harlequin.com

Printed in U.S.A.

Jane Godman is a 2019 Romantic Novelists' Award and National Readers' Choice Award winner and double Daphne du Maurier Award finalist. She writes thrillers for Harlequin Romantic Suspense and also writes paranormal romance. When she isn't reading or writing romance, Jane enjoys cooking, spending time with her family and watching the antics of her dogs, Gravy and Vera.

Books by Jane Godman

Harlequin Romantic Suspense

Colton 911: Grand Rapids
Colton 911: Suspect Under Siege

The Coltons of Mustang Valley
Colton Manhunt

Colton 911
Colton 911: Family Under Fire

The Coltons of Roaring Springs
Colton's Secret Bodyguard

The Coltons of Red Ridge
Colton and the Single Mom

Sons of Stillwater
Covert Kisses
The Soldier's Seduction
Secret Baby, Second Chance

Visit the Author Profile page at Harlequin.com for more titles.

As always, this book is for my lovely husband, Stewart, who is gone but never forgotten. We don't say "goodbye."

Chapter 1

Griffin Colton's job had its highs, lows and harrowing moments. Although his business premises were based in downtown Grand Rapids, his reputation as one of Michigan's best adoption attorneys meant he was in demand across the state. As a result, he spent too many days like the one that had just ended, during which he had been traveling from one courtroom to another.

He loved what he did and wouldn't trade the feeling that came from knowing he'd helped a child find a place with the right family. Even so, by the time he returned to his office for a late-afternoon meeting, his already-low energy levels had drained even further. The leader of the local adoption fundraising organization was passionate in her commitment to securing financial help for families. Griffin agreed to provide leaflets to his clients and direct them to further support if necessary. Although the exchange was productive, it was late when his visitor left, and all Griffin wanted to do was drive the short distance to his Heritage Hill home, order takeout and eat it while watching an old movie.

He was closing down his laptop when his receptionist, Martha Dunne, appeared in the doorway.

"Dr. Abigail Matthews is here to see you." Her expression was apologetic. "I explained that I could make an appointment for another time, but she said it was urgent."

Instinct told Griffin it wasn't a good idea to talk to Abigail. She was the daughter of the man his family were investigating. Colton Investigations was the private firm run by his elder brother, Riley. Griffin and their four sisters—two sets of fraternal twins—took cases only involving a search for justice. The more they investigated banker Wes Matthews and his pyramid scheme involving selling RevitaYou pills the more criminal activity they uncovered. Could Abigail be on a fact-finding mission to discover how much they knew about her dad?

But on the one occasion Griffin had met Abigail Matthews, he'd been touched by her obvious devotion to her nine-month-old foster daughter. Children had always been his weakness, particularly those who were fostered or adopted. Having been in the foster system himself, he could never resist stepping in when there was a child involved.

If Abigail had come to see him because of her baby, it didn't matter who her father was, or what he had done. He would help her.

Without revealing any CI secrets...

"Show her in." He glanced at the clock. "Then go home, Martha. I can lock up here."

When the receptionist returned, she was accompanied by accompanied by Abigail, whose tall, slender frame was dressed in jeans, sneakers and a cotton shirt. Martha indicated for Abigail to step inside, then left. Although his visitor's expression was distracted, Griffin was struck again by her beauty. Her brown hair was streaked blond and hung in waves past her shoulders. With her huge brown eyes, bronze skin, high cheekbones and full lips, she was breathtaking.

Baby Maya was in the stroller and a heavy bag was slung over one of Abigail's shoulders. The look in Abigail's eyes as she focused on Griffin was painful in its intensity.

"Thank you for seeing me..." As she started to hold out her hand, the bag slipped from her shoulder. Diapers, baby wipes, bottles of formula and bags of snacks spilled out across the office floor.

"Oh." Abigail kicked on the stroller's brake and knelt on the rug. Her cheeks flamed as she picked up items and stuffed them back into her bag. "I'm so sorry."

"Hey, it's not a problem," Griffin assured her.

As he squatted close to the stroller to retrieve a bottle of hand sanitizer, Maya leaned forward to get a closer look at him. With her chubby cheeks, brown eyes, and mass of dark curls, the baby was adorable. She gave Griffin a grin followed by a friendly kick to the shoulder. When he pretended to stagger back in pain, she giggled and did it again.

"You might find yourself doing that all day," Abigail said. "Once she finds a game she likes, she wants to play it over and over."

Despite her underlying distress, there was a warm look in her eyes when she looked at Maya that intrigued Griffin. Abigail proclaimed she had no knowledge of her father's crimes. She had even come to Colton Investigations just a few days ago and told him and his siblings about a horrifying discovery that she'd made. Her research had uncovered that there was a compound of ricin in RevitaYou that could be deadly, depending on the person taking it. She believed it was only a matter of time before there were deaths as a result of her father's con.

Yet Griffin's doubts about her lingered. Was it possible that Wes could have funded the development of RevitaYou without the knowledge of his research scientist daughter? Surely she was the first person he would have gone to for advice and support? He couldn't help wondering if this innocent act was an attempt to distance herself from consequences, now that the criminal activity was being uncovered.

Between being kicked by the baby and gathering up stray items that had fallen from the bag, he didn't have any time to pursue that thought. A final glance showed him that most of Abigail's belongings had been restored to her. A flash of pink under his desk caught his eye and he crawled in that direction. As he reached for the knitted teddy bear, his fingers closed over Abigail's and they lightly bumped foreheads.

She clutched the soft toy to her chest. "It's her favorite."

And there it was. That look in the depths of her eyes was what drew him to this job. That need to help his clients and their kids... But it felt like something more this time. It was a little sharper. A touch deeper. He was drawn to Abigail in spite of his reservations about her family.

Griffin got to his feet and held out a hand to help her up. As he did, he was conscious of a damp, sticky feeling in the region of his right knee. He glanced down.

"Mashed banana?"

Abigail bit her lip as she looked at the stain on his suit pants. "You must have knelt on the bag. I'm—"

He grinned. "Sorry? You don't need to keep saying that. Most days my clothes tell the story of my appointments. Paint, ice cream, milkshake..." He pointed to different points on his shirt as he spoke. "My dry cleaning bill would bring tears to your eyes."

For the first time, she managed a slight smile. "I guess it must be one of the hazards of your job."

"And *I* guess that leads us neatly to the question of why you're here?" Griffin went to sit at his desk and indicated one of the chairs on the opposite side.

Before she sat down, Abigail handed the teddy bear to Maya. When she looked back at him, her smile had gone, and her features were tight with tension.

"Maya has been in my care since she was born. Her mom died when she was three months old and it was always my intention to adopt her. This morning, I got a call from my foster care caseworker telling me that my paperwork is being stalled due to an investigation into my fitness to be a parent."

Abigail was struggling to keep her emotions under control. It had taken every ounce of courage she possessed to walk into Griffin Colton's office. She was going to fight for Maya, and to do that she needed help from the best in the business. His professional reputation was well-known. But the reason she had chosen him went deeper.

Abigail had never been under any illusions about her father. Wes Matthews had the looks and charm of a Hollywood idol combined with the heart and soul of a grifter. But his latest fraud had gone too far. When details started to emerge of the RevitaYou pyramid scheme, she had been genuinely surprised that he had kept it secret from her. She was his daughter, and she was a respected clinical pharmaceutical scientist with a reputation as one of the leading independent researchers in the business. Her role involved the discovery and development of new drugs, alongside the improved use of existing medicines. Who better to help Wes keep this new venture on the right side of the law?

Her old insecurities had kicked in. All her life, she'd known she was a disappointment to her dad, who'd made no secret of the fact that he'd wanted a son. For as long as Abigail could remember, she'd been striving to impress him. Her childhood had been a scoreboard on which she'd never gotten enough points. Academically she'd been gifted, getting straight As in every subject. She had never forgotten the time Wes barely glanced at her report card before asking why she wasn't playing more sports. The following year she'd won an athlete-of-the-year award in high school. He turned up late to the presentation, then told her all about his friend's son who was a gifted musician. Now she played piano to concert performance level.

Naturally, she'd believed he hadn't come to her with his plans for RevitaYou because he'd found someone better to provide the clinical support. The old childhood longing for acceptance, never far from the surface, had bubbled up once more. Underneath the hurt, she'd felt a sense of curiosity. What made this wonder drug so special that she wasn't good enough to be part of it? Determined to find out, she'd ordered a thirty-day daily supply of capsules for herself. Although it was not FDA approved, RevitaYou was widely available online.

The pretty green bottle containing the daily vitamin supplement promised to make the lucky user look ten years younger within one week. Instead of swallowing the product, Abigail had taken it into her laboratory and broken it down into its component parts. That was when she'd discovered the awful truth…

"Did your caseworker explain why the process has been stalled?" Griffin's question drew her attention back to the present. Back to the most important part of this whole horrible mess.

Maya. She glanced at her little girl, grounding herself.

I can't lose her.

One thing Wes had taught her about parenting was that she knew what sort of mom she wanted to be. She'd seen all the mistakes and was determined not to make them with her own little girl. Her love for Maya burned fierce and strong, and she clung to it.

The thought gave her the strength she needed to talk about what she'd discovered. And she reminded herself that Griffin already knew all about her father. There would be no surprises for him in the Matthews family background.

"It has to be about my dad." Even though they had to be spoken, the words burned her throat. For an instant, she thought she saw a flare of sympathy in the green depths of Griffin's eyes. But it disappeared within seconds, if it had ever been there at all, and his professional demeanor returned. "About RevitaYou."

"When you came to the CI office a few days ago, you told us that you were not involved in your father's con." Although his voice was nonjudgmental, his gaze probed her face. "You were very determined to make sure that we knew that."

She gave a bitter little laugh. "Are you giving me a chance to retract my statement?"

"Do you need one?"

She shook her head. Hard. "I was not involved in RevitaYou. Not at any stage. The first time I heard about it was when your team started blasting out warnings on social media and I saw the links to my dad. I only knew about it after it was declared potentially toxic." He didn't respond, and she sighed. "I don't know how to convince you that I'm telling the truth."

Griffin was silent for a moment or two, then his gaze dropped to Maya. The baby was rubbing her teddy bear against one cheek, her eyelids drooping sleepily.

"If I represent you, we would be in a unique situation. One that calls for total honesty." He looked back at Abigail. "And the truth is that you can't convince me that you didn't know about your dad's scamming people out of their investments in a toxic supplement." She winced, and he gave her an apologetic smile. "I'm sure you'd rather I told you that up front and moved on to what's important."

She sucked in a breath. "Which is?"

He nodded at Maya. "Your little girl."

For the first time, tears filled her eyes. "Can you help me?"

"I can try." He drew a legal pad and a pen toward him, then pushed a box of tissues toward her. "I need the name of your caseworker and any other details you can give me."

It hadn't occurred to her until now, but Griffin Colton was a very good-looking man. He had the sort of tall, muscular build that fit his expensive designer suit to perfection. And his dark blond hair, sculpted cheekbones and chiseled features were more rock idol than lawyer. But it was those eyes that captured her attention. They were dark green, with the shifting colors and moods of an evening forest. As he smiled, they looked like sunlight on new leaves.

"This may sound like a silly question, but do you mind if I order pizza?" he asked. "If you join me, we can eat while we talk."

"Goodness." An hour later, Abigail looked down at the empty pizza box in surprise. "I didn't even know I was hungry."

Griffin smiled and pointed toward the stroller. "And that little lady has slept through everything."

He liked the way Abigail's face changed when she looked at Maya. It was as if a switch had been flicked and she lit up from within. Had anyone ever looked at him that way? He'd entered the foster system at the age of seven when his mother died. He knew his mom had loved him, and his foster parents, Graham and Kathleen Colton, had cared deeply for him. But *that* look? He wasn't sure he'd ever seen it until now.

"Ah. She likes her sleep." Abigail smoothed down the blanket she'd used to cover the baby's legs. "But she'll wake up hungry."

"It's not relevant to the case, but why did you foster her?"

She was quiet for so long he wasn't sure she was going to answer. When she finally turned away from Maya to look at him, the sadness in her eyes hit him like a punch to his gut. "Maya is my best friend's daughter."

"I'm sorry. This is clearly painful for you—"

She shook her head. "I live with her loss all the time. Talking about it doesn't make it harder. Veronica Pérez and I met in high school. We had a lot in common." A slight smile twisted her lips. "Her parents were from Cuba, and my mother was Cuban, too. Her father worked away a lot. My mom had left my dad by that time and, although I lived with him... Well, I didn't see a lot of him. Veronica and I became each other's family. Our friendship stayed just as strong throughout our adult lives."

As she was talking, her hands twisted in her lap and her eyes focused on a point outside the window. "Sixteen months ago, Veronica came to see me and gave me some devastating news. She had been diagnosed with terminal lung cancer." Abigail turned to look at Maya. "But there was another bombshell. She was also pregnant."

"Her partner...?"

"She didn't have one. Maya was conceived during a drunken one-night stand. When Veronica contacted the father to tell him about the pregnancy, he offered to pay half the cost of an abortion but flatly refused to have anything else to do with the baby. She told him about the cancer, and he said his position hadn't changed."

"Even if he could have been made to accept his parental responsibilities, he doesn't sound like the right person to care for a child." Griffin's expression was grim.

"That's what I said." Abigail nodded her agreement. "And Veronica was an only child with no other family. Her parents had died in a car crash years before. There was no one else."

"Didn't her doctors advise a termination?"

"She wouldn't consider it," Abigail said. "The only treatment available to her was palliative, and she was determined to refuse anything that would affect her baby's chances of survival."

"Even so, you made a life-changing decision when you took her child." The words couldn't adequately express how much his opinion of her had changed. She was Wes Matthews's daughter. As far as the RevitaYou investigation went, that meant he should regard her as the enemy. But Griffin knew how it felt to be ripped out of a home as a child. He knew the damage it had caused to his developing identity. Even though he'd found a loving home with the Coltons, his ability to form bonds had been damaged beyond repair.

That was why Abigail's generous heart touched him so much. She had given Maya everything. A home, a mom, the love every baby so desperately needed. She had given the little girl an identity.

"I didn't have to think about it. Veronica would have done the same for me." She gave a soft laugh. "But you're right. For someone who hadn't given children a thought before this, suddenly becoming a mom *has* been life changing." She pointed to the bulging bag that had been the cause of her earlier embarrassment. "Just getting out of the door is like mounting a polar expedition."

"What happened to Veronica?" He wasn't sure how

tactful it was to ask for details about the brave woman who had carried her baby knowing she wouldn't live to see her grow up.

"She died when Maya was three months old." Abigail hitched in a breath. "Although she was very ill during that time, the three of us got to spend some quality time together. After her death, Maya went through the foster system."

Griffin tapped his pen on the desk. "Presumably, if the adoption has been proceeding, the father has given his permission?"

"Yes. That was agreed while Veronica was still alive." She frowned. "There haven't been any problems. Until now."

"Okay." He was surprised by how much he wanted to make this right. The families were important, of course, but usually his motivation was the child's well-being. This time, his focus was equally divided between Abigail and Maya. He checked the time on his cell phone. "It's late and I may not get an answer but let me see if I can contact your caseworker."

Griffin knew most of the caseworkers in the city and he had a vague recollection of John Jones as a young, earnest man who worked hard for the children in his care.

Although he didn't say it to Abigail, because it sounded boastful, he also knew that his own reputation went before him. If the name Griffin Colton came up on a cell phone display—there wasn't a caseworker alive who would ignore it.

Sure enough, John Jones answered almost immediately. Griffin put him on speakerphone so Abigail could hear the conversation. "Mr. Colton? Hi, what can I do for you, sir?"

"I'm representing Dr. Abigail Matthews. She tells me that the adoption proceedings for her foster daughter, Maya, have been put on hold. I'd like some more details about that decision, please."

He was aware of Abigail's dark gaze fixed on his face as he waited for a reply. In the stroller, Maya murmured quietly in her sleep and waved a chubby hand, as though signifying her own impatience to learn more.

"Um. This is maybe something we should discuss face-to-face." Jones sounded uneasy.

"If the issue is the situation with Dr. Matthews's father, we can talk openly about it."

"No, the RevitaYou situation is not the problem," Jones said. "The reason her paperwork has been put on hold is that I've received information that Dr. Matthews is being investigated as part of her clinical trials to halt the effects of memory loss."

From the way she half rose from her chair, it was clear that this information was news to Abigail. Griffin raised a hand, signaling that he would deal with it. To his relief, although she looked pale and tense, she remained silent.

"Do you have any details about the investigation? And who made the allegation?" he asked.

"I don't have any information about who made the allegations. All I know is that the suggestion is that the doctor has been using an illegal enhancement compound—" There was the sound of Jones turning pages as though he was consulting notes. "A designer, non-FDA-approved drug called Anthrosyne. It appears that, instead of merely halting memory loss, Dr. Matthews has been attempting to boost some of her participants memories in order to gain recognition for her work."

"Can you expand on that?"

"Well, uh… the allegation is that, if Dr. Matthews successfully boosted the memories of her subjects, she would gain considerable attention among her peers. But, of course, she would have been playing with people's lives for her own gain."

Abigail gasped and shook her head but when she tried to speak no sound emerged. Worried for her well-being, Griffin quickly ended his call with the caseworker and went to crouch in front of her.

"Are you okay?"

"It isn't true." She clutched his hand. "There must be some mistake. I'm working on a research project called Mem10, which aims to halt memory loss in Alzheimer's subjects. I've never even heard of Anthrosyne until just now."

"We'll find out what's going on." If this was an act, it was the best he'd ever seen. "But right now, you have something more important that needs your attention."

As he finished speaking, Maya, who had been starting to stir, sat up straight. Hurling her teddy bear to the floor, she gave them an accusing glare and, opening her mouth wide, let out a wail.

Blowing her nose on one of the tissues she still had clutched in her hand, Abigail nodded. "You're right. She comes first. She always will."

Chapter 2

When she had made the decision to foster Maya, Abigail had taken her usual methodical approach to finding the right daycare. She'd created a spreadsheet setting out criteria such as distance from her home and place of work, qualifications of the staff, and reviews. When she'd looked at the website for each place, she'd given each one a score.

By that time, Veronica's illness had been so far advanced that it hurt Abigail to see how frail she was. When Veronica had reached for her hand, and her fingers were so thin, they felt like the delicate claws of a bird.

"How will you score the way they *feel*?" her friend had asked.

Abigail had been slightly bewildered by the question. "Well, I'll go and look at them, of course. I mean, if any of them didn't seem like a comfortable place for a baby..."

Veronica had laughed. "Go take a look at them. Then tell me what you think."

It was only when she'd walked through the doors of the Rainbow Daycare Center that Abigail had understood what her friend had meant. It wasn't the closest to her home or work, but the small center had a warm, welcoming approach that was exactly what she wanted for her daughter. More importantly, Maya loved it as well. And Abigail had ripped up the spreadsheet, a circumstance that had made Veronica smile.

The morning after she'd met with Griffin Colton, Abigail dropped Maya at the center at her usual time. At least she knew that the baby would be well cared for while she tried to untangle what was going on. After a sleepless night, she was eager to get into work and see what she could find out.

For the past five years, she'd worked as a research scientist at the small, private Danvers University. Her most recent project involved leading a clinical trial on participants to test the efficacy of a new memory-boosting, over-the-counter supplement called Mem10. After a long, difficult fight with Alzheimer's, Abigail's paternal grandmother had died from complications of the disease. The personal aspect meant that this was a field that was dear to her heart.

As she drove from the daycare center to the university, she tried, yet again, to make some sense of what John Jones had told Griffin. But there wasn't anything rational about what the caseworker had said. Abigail was in charge of the Mem10 trial. She knew exactly what had gone on at each stage of the process. If it wasn't for the fact that it was impacting the adoption process, she would have dismissed the idea that an illegal compound could have been introduced into the trial as absurd. She found the idea that she would attempt to enhance her reputation in such an underhand way deeply offensive.

Although she couldn't understand why anyone would breach the security of her laboratory or lie about it being breached, she was keen to get in there and double-check her systems and paperwork. As she pulled into her usual place in the parking lot, she was conscious of a few severe glances sent her way, and she squared her shoulders. Working at the university had always been enjoyable, but that had changed when the RevitaYou scandal broke.

These days, Abigail had grown used to getting the evil eye from people who believed she knew all about her father's fraud. She'd had several of her participants' adult children refuse to work with her. A colleague who she'd considered a friend had even confronted her publicly, humiliating her before vowing to never speak to her again.

As far as she knew, none of these people had actually invested in RevitaYou. They simply refused to believe that she wasn't involved.

Determined not to let her father's actions affect her work, she'd overcome her natural reticence and held a meeting to assure her colleagues and participants she knew nothing of her father's pyramid scheme and that she had no idea where he was.

It had been one of the hardest things she'd ever done. Staring at a sea of politely disbelieving faces, she had plowed through her explanation. Although everyone had listened to what she had to say, she knew that she hadn't changed their minds. The realization had hit home. Her name would forever be linked to the RevitaYou scandal.

She had felt it again when she'd met with Griffin. It was obvious that his reaction to her plight had been driven solely by his desire to help Maya. The difference had been Abigail's reaction. She'd wanted to do whatever it took to persuade him of her innocence. . It was only her pride that had made her hold back.

He'd agreed to take her case. She'd secured the best attorney to help her keep Maya. He didn't have to like her or believe in her. So why, when she had so many other things on her mind, did his opinion of her matter so much? The question still occupied her thoughts as she left her vehicle.

"You've got some nerve." someone said from behind her as she walked to her office. The man's voice was soft, but there was no mistaking the menace in his tone.

Abigail swung around sharply. She recognized him immediately. Ryan Thorne was the son of one of her former participants. When the RevitaYou scandal broke, he had withdrawn his father from the Mem10 trial. Although Abigail had tried to persuade him that his dad, Billy, was showing signs of improvement, Ryan had been adamant. He wasn't going to let his dad be experimented upon by a doctor who he thought had been involved in a pyramid scheme.

"Mr. Thorne." She glanced around. The parking lot was quiet and they were all alone. "How's your dad?"

"Not good, thanks to you." He took a step closer.

"I'm sorry to hear that. But you know his place in the program is still open."

He gave a harsh laugh. "You think I'd let you near him again after what I know now?"

"Please believe me, Mr. Thorne. I am not involved in the RevitaYou scheme." As she spoke, another car pulled up close by and she recognized one of her administrative team.

"That line might work with other people. Not me." Thorne threw her a look of disgust. "I've been talking to the others who've withdrawn their parents from your program. You'll get what's coming to you. Just wait and see."

Shoving his hands into his pockets, he stomped away. Shaken, Abigail entered the building and crossed the lobby toward the elevators.

"Dr. Matthews?" Abigail turned to see her boss, Dr. Evan Hardin, standing by the reception desk. His presence in the building a full hour before his usual arrival time was enough to set alarm bells ringing, but the way he used her title instead of her first name worried her most. "Would you come into my office, please?"

Her legs had started to shake so violently that she

had to take a moment to get them under control before she could follow him. Under the interested gaze
of several of her colleagues, she went along the main
corridor in his wake. Following on from her encounter with Ryan Thorne, she wasn't sure she was strong
enough to deal with a confrontation with her boss.

"I'm sorry." Dr. Hardin closed the door behind
him. "There's no easy way to say this. I'm suspend-
ing you pending an investigation into allegations that
you've been using an illegal enhancement compound
as part of the Mem10 trial."

"Evan—" Abigail could barely hear her own voice
for the roaring sound in her ears. "Who made this allegation?"

"I'm not at liberty to divulge that information."

Abigail shook her head from side to side. She had
to know who was responsible for these malicious ru-
mors. If no one would tell her, she'd have to track
down the source on her own. "You can't believe I
would do this."

"It doesn't matter what I think." His face was sympathetic but determined. "I have a duty to the Mem10
program and the participants. Until my investigation
is complete, I can't let you continue to take part in
the trial."

The tremors had taken over her whole body and
Abigail sank into one of the chairs opposite his desk.
Her boss was a kind man, and they'd worked well together over the years. She could tell from his manner that he didn't want to take this action, but he
was right. He couldn't allow his personal feelings

to jeopardize the research—or their subjects. Even so, Mem10 was her project. She overseen its every step. There was so much more than her reputation at stake here.

As Evan handed her a glass of water, she forced herself to focus on the practicalities. "We're at a crucial point. If you halt the program now, it could have a detrimental impact on the outcome."

He lowered his gaze. "I won't halt the program."

Abigail took a sip of water. "What do you mean? You don't have time in your schedule to take over."

"I will appoint a replacement to oversee Mem10 in your absence."

"Oh." Her professional pride shattered into a thousand tiny pieces. At the same time, she thought of the individuals involved the trial, each of whom she had come to know so well. Their lives would be impacted by any change, however minor. "Please choose wisely. There are several competent researchers on my team, but few are qualified to do the role justice."

He lifted his glasses, rubbing his nose wearily. "Thank you for your concern. In addition to this investigation into the illegal use of Anthrosyne, I have another, equally urgent, staffing matter to attend to. If you'll excuse me, Dr. Matthews…"

And that was it. He was no longer using her first name, even in private. It was a polite way of reminding her that she was off the program. And that she should go.

She walked to the door, the shaking in her legs replaced by an unnatural stiffness. Once she was outside and in the corridor, the oddest thought flitted through her head. She really needed to speak to Griffin about this. But why? He was an adoption attorney. He couldn't help her with an employment issue, but most of his siblings were in law enforcement and this was a false allegation. Maybe the CI team could help… She reached into her pocket and drew out her cell, swiping through her address book for his number. As she did, approaching footsteps made her look up.

"Hi, Abigail." The woman approaching gave her a sweet smile. Until recently, Dr. Jenna Avery had been Abigail's closest friend at Danvers University. They'd eaten lunch together each day, gone out for dinner now and then after working late in the lab, even met up at the gym a few times. Then Jenna had confronted Abigail one morning in front of the whole team, hurling abuse at her over RevitaYou. It turned out Jenna was one of the people who'd bought a bottle of the tablets and got sick.

Thanks, Dad. Destroy my reputation. Kill my friendships. Oh, and use your RevitaYou vitamins to poison people for money.

This was the first time Jenna had spoken to Abigail since she'd publicly humiliated her.

"Dr. Hardin has sent for me. I guess he wants me to look after the Mem10 program while you're away." Without waiting for Abigail to reply, Jenna stepped inside Dr. Hardin's office.

It couldn't be true. Jenna Avery was barely competent in her job. Her work was often shoddy, and

Abigail had been forced to challenge her in the past when she'd falsified results. At the time, Abigail had been horrified that Evan had kept Jenna on and had privately wondered if he might be sleeping with her colleague. Those doubts surfaced again now. Jenna wasn't qualified to lead a complex trial like Mem10. Evan must know that…

Choking back a sob, Abigail stuffed her cell back into her pocket and ran from the building. It was only when she reached her car that she realized she hadn't told Evan about Ryan Thorne and his veiled threats.

Griffin had spent the morning in court dealing with four back-to-back cases. By the time the last one was over, he was running late for a meeting with his siblings and he left the court building at a run without pausing to check his messages. Luckily, his office wasn't far from where the Colton Investigations headquarters was located. Once the family home, the mansion on Grand Avenue now belonged to his brother. Although Riley Colton, a former FBI agent, ran CI, Griffin and his sisters contributed their own expertise while working at their full-time jobs.

Since the RevitaYou scandal had hit, and new developments had been breaking almost constantly, the team met more regularly than usual to share information. As he drove the short distance, Griffin reviewed the details of how the story had come to light.

Brody Higgins had been a smart, kicked-around eighteen-year-old foster kid with a small string of misdemeanors when Griffin's dad, Graham, had gotten involved in his case. Brody had been arrested for murder, but Graham had believed the boy was in the wrong place at the wrong time and declined to prosecute. The decision, and subsequent capture of the real killer, had solidified the name of Graham Colton as a hero in Michigan. It also helped turn Brody's life around. Since then, the Coltons had looked out for Brody and treated him like family.

Now aged twenty-seven and a law school graduate, Brody had only wanted a high-paying corporate job and the good life. So it had come as a surprise to Riley when he turned up at his office the previous month looking nervously over his shoulder. The explanation for his behavior was that a big-time loan shark was after him. He'd borrowed five thousand dollars to get in on a can't-fail product called Revita-You. The vitamin supplements claimed to turn back the clock ten years and the drug was so new that the FDA hadn't even seen it yet.

Although Riley had been incredulous that anyone could have fallen for this illegal pyramid scheme, Brody explained that he happened to pass by a promo for a seminar about making six figures overnight by becoming a member of the exclusive RevitaYou "team" that invested in the product, recruited new members and sold the vitamins. He'd gone along to the seminar where he met real people, including a scientist, four other investors and people who took the vitamins for just two weeks. They produced amazing before and after photos, and gave testimonials raving about the product.

Brody had wanted to pay back his huge law school loans and impress his older girlfriend. He'd felt so sure about RevitaYou that he borrowed the money to invest from an anonymous group called Capital X. Riley in particular had heard about the dangerous operation from the FBI but had never been able to bust them. Capital X used a unique incentive to get their clients to pay up on time. If any payment, including the very high interest, was late, Capital X goons would break two bones at a time until the outstanding amount was paid.

Riley's blood had run cold when Brody showed him his left hand. The ring finger and pinky had been bandaged together. To make things worse, Brody had given his girlfriend a bottle of RevitaYou as a gift, hoping to recruit her to sell the product because he'd get extra bonuses. Instead of being impressed, she'd dumped him. Not only had RevitaYou left her looking ten years *older* but she'd been sick for two days after taking it. Apparently, she was still having issues that seemed to be related to the vitamins. In the light of Abigail's later discovery about ricin, it seemed that Brody had handed his girlfriend a bottle of poison.

Brody had immediately called Wes Matthews, the guy who'd taken his money in cash transfers, to demand his investment back and report the problems with the product. Wes had emailed back that he never received the money and that Brody must be mistaken. After that, Wes, and the whole RevitaYou operation, including the fancy website, had disappeared.

The timing of Brody's recklessness couldn't have

been worse. The CI team didn't have five minutes to spare; all his siblings were all busy. But this was Brody, so Riley had called an emergency meeting of his siblings to discuss next steps. Brody, who had agreed to go into a safe house, hadn't shown up for the meeting and sent a message to let the Coltons know he had gone into hiding. While he was concerned for Brody's safety, Griffin felt it was typical of the younger man to run away from his problems.

Traffic up ahead was at a standstill and Griffin leaned back in his seat.

"Feels like stepping back in time." The murmured words were a reference to his feelings about Brody and the way it felt like everyone sprang to attention whenever *he* needed help. On one level, Griffin knew he was too hard on Brody, on another, he felt like someone had to be. And, to be fair, Brody never resented that slight distance between them.

He sighed. But it wasn't like stepping back in time. Brody could be in real trouble this time. And, no matter, how much Griffin resented the easy attention Brody received within the family group, he didn't want to see him get hurt.

Griffin had been reluctant to get involved this time around. He'd insisted Brody should have known better than to get involved in a pyramid scheme and with a loan shark. Sometimes, the support his family had given to Brody had grated with him, even though there was no reason why it should. His feelings of isolation were his own issue rather than anything to do with the way he was treated within his family. Ever since his birth mother had been killed, he'd felt alone.

He was honest enough to admit that, but it didn't change anything. He still thought Brody got preferential treatment. Griffin knew he'd been cared for and loved as much as any member of the family. But Brody's personality meant he liked an easy ride and these problems he was having now were part of that. If the Coltons had been tougher with Brody when he was younger, maybe things would have turned out differently.

The vehicles in front were moving and he straightened, glad of a break from his thoughts.

In the end, the search for justice—always uppermost with the Coltons—had prevailed. The siblings all wanted con artist Wes Matthews caught before he could steal from more people. Despite his reservations about stepping in to save Brody from his own foolishness, Griffin had said he was in, and they'd taken on the case to honor their dad's memory.

As he pulled into the drive of the house that had been his home since he was eight, Griffin reflected that they couldn't have known at that point how quickly things would escalate. The last they'd heard from Brody was a text from a burner phone, telling them that the Capital X henchmen were on his tail. Right now, they had no idea whether he was dead or alive.

As if Brody's troubles and the subsequent Revita-You commotion wasn't enough to occupy his mind, Griffin's thoughts had been turning toward Abigail

Matthews throughout the day. It was an inconvenience he could do without. Still not convinced of her innocence in the RevitaYou con, he couldn't allow himself to be drawn in by her plight. Particularly as he wasn't even sure it was her difficulties that were the reason he wanted to get involved. For the first time in as long as he could remember, he had felt a powerful attraction to a woman. And *that* wasn't happening.

Just as he was reminding himself of that, his cell rang. Bringing his vehicle to a halt, he reached into his jacket pocket and drew out his phone. He checked the name on the display. *Abigail Matthews.* A glance around the drive told him his sisters were already there. He didn't have time to take the call. He should let it go to voice mail, but there was no way he was keeping Abigail waiting.

"Griffin Colton."

"I got suspended from my job today." He could tell she was crying.

Griffin studied the facade of the beautiful old house as he took a moment to consider the issues. Bringing Wes Matthews to justice had started out as a campaign for justice but it had spiraled into something bigger. As the scale of the con became clear, it had turned into a crusade on behalf of each individual who had lost their cash, their health or both.

Abigail's role in RevitaYou was still unclear. Had she been involved and was now trying to paint herself as an innocent dupe? It was always possible that she had genuinely been unaware of her father's exploits and was trying to help him now, but could he afford to be open-minded about that? If she was attempting to infiltrate CI to find out what they knew he couldn't let her get too close. His brother and sisters certainly wouldn't allow it.

And the story about being framed for using an illegal drug? Was that just another layer in the con? Could he believe anything she told him?

But the pain in her voice was real. And it was not something he could ignore. She might be a complication. He might not want her in his life but he felt responsible for her. She had come to him for help, and he wasn't going to let her, or Maya, down.

"I'm at the CI headquarters. Meet me here."

It wouldn't be the first time he'd been out of step with his siblings.

It was only when she thought about going to the CI headquarters that Abigail stopped to consider what she was doing. And more importantly about what *Griffin* was doing. She didn't think for a minute that his invitation was an indication that he, or his siblings, believed in her innocence. It might even be a way of drawing her in so they could find out more out about her dad and his whereabouts. If they only knew the truth. His daughter was the last person in whom Wes would confide.

She had never felt so scared or alone. Her mom had died when she was thirteen, but she hadn't seen her for many years before that, and her dad had hardly been a nurturing figure. Seeing her best friend die only months before had been hard enough, but now, she also faced the prospect of losing her career and maybe even Maya, all through no fault of her own. Her name had already been tarnished through association with her father's misdeeds. Now, she was being accused of skewing the results of her trial to boost her own reputation. Who would believe she was innocent?

When she had arrived home that morning, after collecting Maya from daycare, she had sent a quick email to Dr. Hardin.

It may be nothing, but I was confronted today by Ryan Thorne, the son of a former Mem10 participant. He is very angry about my perceived involvement in RevitaYou and said he had been in contact with the families of other former participants. He said I would "get what's coming." His anger seems to be directed against me personally but I thought you should be aware.

Although she had copied the email to the university HR department, she had no real idea where the allegations against her had come from and who was making them. Until she found more information, she couldn't begin to build a defense. Frustrated, hurt and disbelieving, she had called Griffin in the hope that he had heard something more from John Jones. When he suggested meeting him at the CI headquarters, she'd been so relieved at the thought of seeing someone who was on her side, she'd have agreed to anything. It was only when she ended the call that she questioned her decision.

Because... *On her side?* Were those really the right words to describe Griffin?

She had gone to him because of his professional reputation. In her situation, she couldn't take any chances. Losing Maya wasn't an option. But these latest developments were making her question her decision to choose a Colton. If the CI team believed she was guilty of assisting in the RevitaYou con, her suspension from her job would give them additional ammunition against her.

Griffin had been sympathetic toward her, and she believed he had been genuine when he said he wanted to help her keep Maya. But he wouldn't break with his siblings. Of that she was sure.

So, right now, stepping inside would be a little like walking into enemy territory. For the second time.

The first time, she'd dashed headlong into the beautiful old house, determined to let the Colton siblings know what she'd discovered about RevitaYou. Even though it reflected badly on her dad, they had to know that there was a deadly compound in the vitamins. Acting on a hunch, she had ordered a bottle of RevitaYou and, instead of swallowing the pills, taken them into her laboratory and analyzed their component parts. That was when she had discovered the truth. So many people were ingesting a poison. It was only a matter of time before deaths would result.

Abigail wanted to tell the world she didn't believe her father would be behind such an awful scheme.

But that would be a lie. The truth was, if he thought it would make him money, he was capable of anything. His personal life had always been a reflection of his business dealings. She remembered her mom, Sofia Barroso, as a sweet, beautiful woman. When she realized what a cold-hearted, conniving man Wes really was, Sofia had left him. Although she had tried to get custody of Abigail, who had been ten at the time, Wes had determinedly fought her and kept her away from her daughter. Sofia had died three years later in a car accident. Wes never remarried and, although he'd dated, his relationships never lasted. Abigail realized later that his self-absorption meant he was unable to feign an interest in another person for long.

Abigail couldn't share the outrage most people evidently felt when Wes had gone into hiding instead of facing his accusers. It was exactly the behavior she'd expect of him. If he didn't look good, he'd walk away. And he certainly wouldn't stick around to face prosecution. Life behind bars? That wouldn't suit Wes Matthews.

None of this soul-searching was helping in her decision about whether she should go ahead and meet with Griffin. Would she be better finding another attorney? Someone who had no preconceptions about her and her father? Someone whose last name wasn't Colton?

She had almost made up her mind to call Griffin and tell him she wouldn't be meeting him, when Maya woke up from her nap. Abigail had tucked her into the crib in the living room, noticing, as she did, how much the baby had grown. Soon, she'd be too big for the cradle next to Abigail's desk…

The thought brought a panicky lump to her throat. If Abigail couldn't adopt her, who would be there to oversee the milestones in Maya's life? She had to be the one. At first, she'd loved the little girl because she was a link to Veronica. She had made a promise to her friend and had been determined to see it through. Over time, that had changed, and she had fallen in love with Maya for her own sake. Now she was Maya's mom. She couldn't imagine the world without her little girl in it.

As if reacting to Abigail's fears, the little girl reached up her plump arms and gave a beaming smile. Even though Veronica had lived for a few months after giving birth, she'd made sure Maya always viewed Abigail as her mom. The extensive palliative treatment she was undergoing, together with the fact that she knew she wouldn't be around to care for her daughter, meant she wanted to make sure Maya identified right from the start with the parent who'd be there. Although it had broken Abigail's heart, she'd known her friend had been right.

Now, as she lifted Maya from the crib and held her warm, sweetly scented weight against her shoulder, love surged through her, reigniting her strength and resolve. Her life had spun wildly off course recently. She didn't know why, and events had been out of her control. But starting now, she was going to fight back. Maya, her job and her reputation were all too important for her to give up on.

There was only one person she trusted right now. She didn't know why, since his role in the RevitaYou investigation automatically made him suspicious of her. But Griffin Colton appeared to have an aura of integrity, and he'd said he would do his best to help her.

"I guess that's as good a place to start as any," she told Maya, as she gathered up the baby's bag, together with her cell phone and car keys.

Chapter 3

Griffin entered the house through the door at the rear, which took him straight into the family kitchen. He could hear voices coming from the formal dining room and guessed the rest of the team had already gathered around the table in preparation for the meeting. As he approached the room, Pal, Riley's German shepherd, scurried up and thrust a wet nose into his hand.

"Good girl." Griffin patted her head and the dog immediately flopped over onto her back, inviting him to tickle her belly. "Sorry. I don't have time." He lowered his voice. "I'm already about to make myself unpopular."

"Griffin?" His sister Sadie gave him a smirk as he entered the room. "We thought you weren't coming."

"That's not fair. Or funny." Her fraternal twin, Vikki, gave her a reproachful look. "We've all been late now and then."

"Except Riley," Pippa pointed out.

"That's not surprising," Kiely, Pippa's twin, laughed. "He lives here."

Riley looked up from the electronic tablet he'd been studying. "Plus, I'm the responsible one, re-member?"

Although there was a twinkle in his eye, Griffin knew there was a world of meaning behind the words. As the oldest of six children, Riley had grown up with a sense of responsibility. His father's career had been time-consuming and required a lot from both his parents, which meant many of the daily parent-ing duties had fallen to Riley. He had often been ex-pected to babysit, to mentor them, support them with homework and help out with sports and other hobbies. He had the same opportunities as the others, but he'd also done his share of caring.

The former FBI agent was forty-three and Griffin had figured he'd been determined to remain single. In the last few weeks, however, events had taken an unexpected turn. Riley had protected social worker Charlize Kent, with whom he'd had a one-night fling, when she was in danger. Now Riley and Charlize were engaged and expecting a baby and Charlize had moved in with Riley. Griffin was delighted for his brother, but the change in Riley's circumstances once again highlighted his own isolation.

Although he dated, Griffin had never had a close

relationship with a woman. In the same way that he was welcomed into the family group, but slightly apart from it, he figured it was to do with his reluctance to show his feelings.

Griffin took a seat at the table and was grateful for the cup of black coffee Sadie pushed in his direction.

"Strong enough that it could have come out of a volcano. Just the way you like it." She gave him a sympathetic smile. "Rough morning?"

"Is there any other kind?"

Sadie, a crime scene investigator with an equally heavy workload, nodded her agreement. Since Riley seemed about ready to start the meeting, they turned their attention his way.

"Let's start with the most important thing… Has anyone heard from Brody?" Riley didn't appear hopeful as he looked at each of his siblings in turn. There was a collective shaking of heads in response. "Pippa, you're the one he was always closest to. He may contact you first."

"I've tried texting him a few times," Pippa said. "But he doesn't reply."

"Clearly, he's still lying low and is terrified about what the Capital X goons will do if they catch up with him." Riley tapped a finger on the table. "All we can do is keep trying to get in touch with him and also attempt to find out more about Capital X."

"Do we have any new information about other aspects of the investigation since our last meeting?" Griffin asked.

Riley consulted the notes on his screen. "We know

that Detective Emmanuel Iglesias of the GRPD has opened a RevitaYou case file. I've been sharing information with him. Before Brody came to see me, sixteen people had come forward to say they believed they'd been conned into investing in Wes Matthews's pyramid scheme. Brody was number seventeen and Charlize's aunt, Blythe, was the eighteenth." He looked up. "What about Capital X? Griffin, you'd been looking into them."

Griffin shook his head. Although the CI team was committed to breaking open the underground loan operation, Capital X had proved good at covering its tracks. "I only have what I've already shared. They seem to have unlimited capital because of their brutal tactics and interest rates. They operate underground and on the dark web. No one knows who runs the operation. Everything is anonymous and everyone uses burner phones."

"There must be a way to get in there." Kiely frowned impatiently. She was a freelance private investigator, and Griffin could almost see her formulating plans to get information about the shadowy organization.

"We'll keep trying to find a way," Riley said.

"This stuff is poison." Pippa wrinkled her nose, the expression a reflection of how the family felt about the dangerous vitamins. "And that fits with what Wes Matthews's own daughter told us. There is a ricin compound in the tablets and it's only a matter of time before someone dies."

"What about Abigail Matthews?" JAG attorney

Vikki cast a quick glance around the table. "Has anyone checked her out? I find it hard to believe she didn't know what was going on, or that she doesn't know where her dad is now."

Griffin glanced at his watch. Even allowing for time to get Maya ready, Abigail would be there soon. It was time to speak up...

"Dr. Matthews is on her way over."

The five pairs of eyes that turned to look his way pinned him in place the same way the family cat used to fix its prey before it pounced. Griffin had never felt like a real Colton, but he'd never wished he wasn't part of the family unit. Right now, he wasn't quite so sure if he still felt that way.

"You mean you've asked her here because she has more information for us, is that right?" Although Riley was offering him a way to help out the team, his brother didn't sound hopeful.

"I didn't ask her for that reason. She was suspended from her job today and I don't think she has anywhere else to go for help right now." Under their skeptical gazes, he quickly outlined the details of his meeting with Abigail, the investigation into her alleged use of Anthrosyne in the Mem10 program and its impact on her adoption of Maya.

"You realize that none of this makes her appear more trustworthy?" Sadie asked. "If anything, it reinforces the idea that she's likely to be as unprincipled as her father. If she wouldn't hesitate to use an illegal substance in one drug she's trialing, why would she think twice when it came to RevitaYou?"

"Whoa." Griffin held up a hand. "Firstly, the allegation against her is just that. Nothing has been proved and the Anthrosyne investigation hasn't even started. Secondly, Abigail is the person who came to us with the information that there is a ricin compound in RevitaYou. Why would she do that if she was responsible for putting it there? Why wouldn't she have gone into hiding with her dad?"

Even though his questions were greeted with silence, he could tell he wasn't convincing anyone. Why would his family buy into her innocence when he wasn't sure about Abigail himself? It was a strange situation but, even though he had his doubts, he wasn't prepared to let anyone else make a judgment before they had all the facts. To be fair, his brother and sisters, having been raised with such a strong belief in justice, were equally unlikely to jump to unfair conclusions.

Despite that, Kiely couldn't resist voicing a concern. "What if telling us about the ricin was a ruse to make us think she wasn't involved in RevitaYou? If we believe her, she escapes prosecution and keeps her career and reputation. It also raises the possibility that she can get information from us to find out what's happening with our investigation." She gave Griffin an apologetic look. "If Abigail gains the confidence of someone on the inside, she could relay confidential information back to her father."

There was murmur of protest around the table. "None of us would share details of a case unless we were sure it was okay to do so," Riley said.

"I'm sorry." Kiely reached across to place her hand over Griffin's. "I didn't mean to suggest that you would."

"I know you didn't." As he returned the grip of her fingers, Griffin reflected that this was all part of his dilemma. By supporting Abigail, he was risking more than an attraction that pulled him out of his comfort zone. The reality was that he shouldn't take her case. No matter how sorry he felt for her, or how much he wanted to help Maya find a permanent home, this situation was too complicated. Even if Abigail had had no knowledge of what her father had done, they were on opposite sides here. And he couldn't foresee a good outcome from that.

The tense atmosphere was interrupted when Pal started barking, signaling that someone was on the premises. Clients and other visitors had to park on the street and walk up the long driveway. Griffin got up from his seat and was heading out into the hall when there was a knock on the front door.

With his emotions in turmoil, he went to open it. After the conversation he'd just had, did he even want to see Abigail again? If there was even the slightest chance that she could come between him and his family, the answer had to be no. At the same time, his heart was racing at the thought of being able to do something to help her.

When he opened the door and saw her face, his doubts vanished. She was pale, with dark circles under her eyes, her hair was untidy, and there was a stain on her lapel that looked like dried oatmeal. She was still the most beautiful woman he'd ever seen. And there was no way he could believe that her behavior was an act to dupe him into revealing information about the RevitaYou investigation.

Maya, who appeared to be full of life, greeted him with a wide grin, then held out her arms as though he was a long-lost friend.

"Can I hold her?" Griffin asked.

"Oh, please do." Abigail handed the baby over. "She's getting heavy now, and today's been..." Her lip wobbled. "I'm sorry."

"Hey." Shifting Maya into the crook of his right elbow, he slid his left arm around Abigail. She leaned gratefully against him as he drew her into the house. "I can only imagine how tough it's been." He paused. "My family are all here. Is that going to be too difficult for you to handle right now?"

She remained still for a moment or two with her head resting on his shoulder, then she straightened. When she looked up, her expression was determined. "I'm ready to see them. Why wouldn't I be? I have nothing to hide."

Although she'd said she was ready to face Griffin's family, Abigail experienced a moment of near panic as she followed him into the large dining room where the Colton siblings were assembled. It was the same room in which she'd met with them when she'd rushed to tell them her findings about the ricin compound she'd discovered in RevitaYou. She had no regrets about sharing that information, but she knew the CI team had questioned her motives.

Everyone questions my motives.

And she didn't really blame people. It was unfair, and it hurt, but she could understand how she must look to anyone who didn't know her. And, now that Veronica was dead, there was no one with whom she was really close. Loneliness and grief squeezed her heart until she wanted to cry out for the pain to stop. Instead, she held her head a little higher and faced Griffin's brother and sisters.

"Dr. Matthews." Riley Colton got to his feet and indicated an empty chair. "Griffin has been telling us about the problems you've been experiencing."

Abigail sat down and Griffin took the chair next to hers with Maya in his lap. The baby, clearly deciding that all of these people had assembled just to see her, clapped her hands and waved. The gesture broke the ice a little as everyone laughed and Griffin's sisters returned the waves. Overwhelmed by this response, Maya buried her face in Griffin's shirt front and played with the end of his tie.

"I don't know if anyone will believe me, but I did not use an illegal compound to enhance my subjects' memories." There. Saying the words out loud made her feel stronger and strengthened her determination to clear her name. "And I don't know who is trying to frame me."

She wasn't sure if her conviction swayed anyone in the room, but no one looked away or was openly hostile. Pippa Colton, who was an attorney, leaned forward. "But we can assume that this non-FDA-approved substance *has* been used as part of your program?"

"What are you getting at?" Griffin frowned at his sister.

"It's a simple enough question," Pippa said. "If the Anthrosyne drug has definitely been used, but Abigail wasn't responsible for it, the investigators need to take a broad approach to their inquiry."

"Of course." Griffin turned to Abigail. "The Anthrosyne investigation should consider the possibility that someone else could have introduced this substance into the program."

"But I'm in charge of the Mem10 trial." Abigail was confused by the suggestion that anyone else could have intervened. "I don't understand what another person would have to gain from using an illegal compound in this way. It's my name that would be on the research papers."

"If someone else was involved, maybe the motive would become clear when that person's identity was uncovered?" Griffin suggested.

"It's possible, I suppose." Abigail remained skeptical. She had a small team of part-time research scientists who had assisted her with the Mem10 trial since its inception two years earlier. Most of them were dedicated to the university and to the projects in which they were involved. She couldn't imagine a situation in which any of them would risk damaging a piece of work in this way. More importantly, she could see no reason for them to do it.

"I know this isn't a good time to ask you this—" Riley cleared his throat.

Abigail knew what was coming. "You want to know if I've heard from my father?" She shook her head. "It's hard to explain but…" She felt there was a chance she might be able to make this group of people understand her relationship with her father. They seemed prepared to listen to her and, for some reason, she sensed they were trying hard not to judge her. "My dad and I aren't close. I'm probably the last person he'd get in touch with."

"Even so, without consciously knowing where he is, you could have some clues about where he may have gone," Griffin said. "You may have overheard him talking about places he's been to, contacts he has, even other countries he wanted to visit. There's no reason why he would stay in America. In fact, it would make sense for him to get as far away as possible."

"I've been going over and over those things in my mind, but I can't think of anything." As she spoke, Abigail's breathing became more rapid and shallow. Her chest tightened as though a hurricane was building inside her. Was this what a panic attack felt like? Because all she wanted to do right now was snatch up Maya and flee.

"It's okay." Griffin placed a hand over hers and his warm, strong touch restored some of her calm. "No one is asking you to come up with answers here and now. But something may come to you. If it does, you know where to find us."

She bent her head, feeling some of the anxiety recede. He was right. The sense of urgency she felt was being driven by everything that was going on in her life, but it had no basis in fact. Although it would be helpful to the CI team and the Grand Rapids police to find her father quickly and get the answers to their questions, it didn't have to happen right this minute. This feeling that she couldn't breathe until things were resolved was caused by stress, not reality.

When she looked up and met Griffin's gaze, she saw a measure of understanding in the green depths of his eyes. She couldn't tell whether he knew the direction of her thoughts or simply guessed that she was hurting and wanted to help. Either way, she was glad of his comforting presence.

The conversation continued around her and she was grateful to the Colton siblings for speaking freely about the RevitaYou investigation. Their frustration and distaste was obvious. They clearly could not comprehend a mindset such as her father's. Wes Matthews had always placed his love of money and material things above all other considerations. Even, it had now become clear, the law.

The meeting ended with Riley and his siblings discussing his meeting with two elderly couples who had invested in RevitaYou. Ellis and Reva Layne and John and Cassie Winslow had no idea where Wes could have gone and had gained no clues from anything the man said to them.

"At least I took their story to the local news station," Riley said. "I gave a reporter details of the

RevitaYou scam, the sickness caused by the tablets and the disappearance of banker Wes Matthews. The anchor interviewed Detective Emmanuel Iglesias on camera, and he was able to give a warning not to take the product."

"It still doesn't get us any further along," Sadie sighed. "It feels like we've stalled when it comes to finding Matthews and cracking open Capital X."

"I could do some more searching and see if I can find more about who else has worked with my dad on the RevitaYou formula," Abigail offered. "He's not a chemist. Someone had to come up with the formula for the pills."

"That would be helpful," Griffin said.

Maya had been happily tugging on his tie and peeping through her fingers at his siblings. Now, she was getting restless and started to wriggle to be put down.

"It's getting close to her dinnertime." Abigail held out her arms, and Maya launched herself toward her. "I should take her home."

"I'll see you out." Griffin got to his feet and helped her up from her chair.

"I hope you'll feel able to join us at our next meeting, Dr. Matthews—" Riley broke off with a slight smile. "And perhaps we should use first names from now on?"

She managed a smile. "Yes. Call me Abigail. And I hope I'll have more information for you next time we meet."

Griffin escorted her out into the hall and opened the front door. "I hope that wasn't too difficult?"

"In a strange way, it was useful." She frowned as she tried to find the words to express what she meant. "I can see how hard you and your family are working to make this right and I want to help. I still find it hard to believe that my dad is the person responsible for all of this." She looked out at the driveway. "I just…"

He waited for a few moments before prompting her. "You just…?"

"On top of everything else, I was threatened by the son of one of my participants today."

"You need to go to the police." His expression was concerned. "Threats can turn nasty."

She shook her head. "It wasn't an explicit threat. Hopefully once the group who object to me because of RevitaYou know I'm off the Mem10 trial, they'll forget their objections and get back on board. I just don't want to be alone with my thoughts tonight. Once Maya is asleep, I know I'll keep going over and over this allegation."

"How about I finish up here and then come by your place with takeout?"

She looked at him in surprise. "You don't have to do that."

"I know I don't have to. I want to." He patted Maya's cheek. "You get this little one home and I'll see you in a few hours."

Unable to speak because of the lump in her throat, Abigail nodded. His kindness had caught her unawares once again and, as she headed toward her car, all she could think was how nice it would have been to have discovered this sweet side of his nature in different circumstances.

Chapter 4

Griffin had a mountain of reading to get through for a court case. He also had an early start the following day and he needed a good night's sleep. So why was he bringing dinner over to Abigail's house, wondering what sort of food she liked and agonizing over whether he should take wine or beer? He knew nothing about this woman. Actually, that wasn't true. He knew plenty about her—just not about her tastes.

Yet his instinct persisted. He wanted to help and protect her. Damn it. He didn't even know if she drank alcohol. He added soda to the order on the delivery app he used, then returned his cell phone to his pocket and, having saved his files, closed down his laptop.

He didn't understand what was going on. His natural caution had deserted him and, in its place there was a fizzing excitement that he'd never experienced before. Even when he should be thinking about other things, Abigail intruded into his thoughts. He'd never had a crush, not one that had lasted more than a day or two, but he imagined it felt a lot like this. Out of all the women he could have been attracted to, he had to choose the most unsuitable one. At thirty-two years of age, he was seeing the emotions over which he'd always exercised such tight control rebel in spectacular style.

He'd sometimes wondered if the timing of his adoption was the key to his feelings of isolation. Although he was still young when he'd been brought into the Colton family, he'd been old enough to already have an identity, a sense of who he was. The sense of difference came from within, not from anything imposed by his adoptive family.

Surely this change was a good enough reason *not* to go over to Abigail's place. After spending his whole life feeling like he didn't fit in, Griffin was always afraid that in his personal relationships he would either be too distant, or that his craving for love would overpower a partner. As a result, he dated, but never allowed himself get close to a woman. This attraction he felt toward Abigail was stronger than anything he'd ever known. Could he rely on his usual self-restraint?

At the same time, the urge to see her again was overwhelming. And, just for once, he wanted to stop being cautious. Just for once, he wanted to act on impulse and see where it led him. Snatching up his car keys, he headed out of his apartment door before discretion took over again.

His apartment was close to the CI headquarters but Abigail lived in a small house near the Danvers University campus where she worked. The drive took about twenty minutes, during which time Griffin grew impatient. Having made up his mind that he wanted to see her, he was in a hurry to get over to her place. She had impressed him earlier with her resilience, but there was no doubt about the tough time she was having. Other than helping with the adoption case, he wasn't sure what else he could do. But he knew for sure that he wanted to try. If he could lift some of the burden from those slender shoulders and take the haunted look from her eyes, he would.

He knew what his siblings would say. Griffin had always identified with the underdog. Possibly it was why he resented Brody, who had an air of expectation about him. Probably because of his own difficult start in life, Griffin wanted to support those who were struggling to help themselves. Abigail wasn't weak, but the odds were stacked against her in every part of her life right now. Was that the root of this attraction? Was he drawn to her because of her vulnerability?

When she answered her front door, he almost laughed out loud at the question. In that instant, his feelings for her had nothing to do with her fragility, or her need for protection. They had a lot to do with the fact that Abigail Matthews was *gorgeous*. Then she smiled, and he got the first clue that this might be something more than a physical attraction. Putting his heart out there wasn't going to be part of the deal.

"Maya finally fell asleep about half an hour ago," she said, as he stepped inside a small hall. "She was tired, but she wouldn't settle."

"She can probably sense your mood." Griffin followed her into a small, cozy kitchen and dining room.

Abigail nodded. "She's had such a difficult start in life. I always try so hard to keep things light, but babies are very intuitive." Her lip wobbled slightly, and she sucked in a breath. "I'm all she has, so she's bound to pick up on how I'm feeling."

"Hey." He placed a hand on her arm. "Maya is a very lucky little girl. She's loved. Sadly, I see many instances of kids who are not."

"Oh, goodness." Her eyes were troubled as she scanned his face. "That must be so difficult for you to deal with."

It was almost a shock to realize that she got it. For the first time ever, someone understood, without being told, that Griffin didn't do a bland nine-to-five desk job. His siblings had an idea about the heartbreak he saw on a daily basis. Otherwise, no one appreciated that he spent most of his time trying to undo tragedy.

For an instant, his throat tightened, and he didn't trust himself to respond. Instead, he turned the conversation to a safer direction. "I ordered the takeout to be delivered here. I hope you like Chinese food?"

"Love it." She smiled. "And, in spite of everything that's been happening, I'm hungry."

He checked his cell phone. "It should be here in a few minutes."

"Just enough time to get ready."

She moved quickly around the kitchen. Reaching into cupboards and drawers, she handed Griffin plates, glasses and forks, which he placed on the small table. Just as Abigail was filling a jug with water, there was a knock on the door.

"Perfect timing." They shared a smile before she headed to answer it. When she returned, she pretended to stagger under the weight of the brown paper bags she was carrying. "How many people are you expecting?"

Griffin laughed. "My family will tell you that I always overcater."

"That's okay. I love leftovers for breakfast." She hesitated, apparently aware that her words could have held a double meaning. "That is… I don't know if… What I meant was…"

Griffin came to her rescue. "Don't count on there being any leftovers. I haven't eaten all day, and that smells good."

She gave him a grateful smile. "It sure does."

They sat at the table and spent the next few minutes opening the various cartons and piling food onto their plates.

"I didn't know what you'd want to drink." Griffin indicated the selection of beer, wine and soda.

"I don't usually drink on a work night—" She gave a little gasp as she realized what she'd said, then shrugged. "But I guess that won't be a problem, so I'll take a beer."

Her attempt at lightheartedness didn't quite work. As he reached for one of the chilled bottles, Griffin caught a glimpse of the hurt in her eyes. It seemed impossible to believe that if she had been responsible for using the illegal substance in her research, she would be so shocked and hurt at the treatment she was getting.

His head might be telling him to be wary around Abigail, but his heart was giving him a different message. He had been brought up in a family that had a strong emphasis on care and support. It had been one of the biggest motivators in his life. He had come late to being a Colton, but he didn't walk away from people who needed his help.

"Have you heard any more from your boss?" he asked. "They should move quickly on this Anthrosyne investigation. Keeping you waiting would be unfair."

"I had an email confirming the decision to suspend me and outlining the reasons. It didn't tell me anything that I don't already know." Although her expression was gloomy, he was glad to see her scoop up a forkful of rice and start eating.

"And do you have legal representation? I can help you with the adoption case, but I have no experience with employment law."

"I guess that's the next step," she sighed. "I know nothing about this sort of thing. I wouldn't know where to start looking for a decent attorney."

"Leave it to me." He pushed a carton of chop suey in her direction. "My sisters will know someone, particularly Pippa, who is an attorney."

She bent her head over her plate. "Will this affect my chances of keeping Maya?"

"The fact that you are under investigation for a serious misdemeanor, one that could potentially lead to a criminal charge, is already impacting the adoption process. That's why we need your employer to get the Anthrosyne investigation completed quickly." He didn't want to give her any false hope, but he felt confident in his next statement. "You shouldn't worry that anything will happen immediately. That fact that you are under investigation will not be enough for Maya to be removed from your care."

"What—" She fiddled with the label on her beer bottle before taking a slug. "What about RevitaYou? Most people think I was involved in that, too."

"But you weren't." As he said it, he knew he believed it. "Which means there's no real evidence against you. This is Maya's home. She won't be taken away from you over some unfounded allegations."

When she finally met his gaze, he saw a sheen of tears in her eyes. "Thank you."

They ate in silence for a few minutes, then Abigail returned to the subject of Griffin's job. "I would imagine it can be rewarding as well as emotionally draining."

"It can. There's nothing quite like that feeling of knowing you've helped a child find the right family."

"What made you choose that career?" she asked.

He didn't usually talk about his early life. These days, no one ever questioned his status as a Colton. When he was younger, if the subject ever arose, his adoptive parents, Graham and Kathleen, would always reassure him about how loved and wanted he was. And he'd always wanted to believe them...

"I was taken into foster care at the age of seven after my mom was killed by her abusive partner." He wasn't sure he'd *ever* said those words out loud.

"Oh, my goodness." Abigail reached out and took his hand. "How terrible for you."

"I listen to people now who speculate about how much a child of that age can remember, and I want to tell them to rip up their books and studies and start over again. Because I remember everything about my mom," Griffin said. "I know how she looked, how she smelled, and the clothes she wore. I can hear her voice, her laughter. I remember the stories she told me, the songs we sang together. I can still taste her awful cooking." He laughed. "Do I really remember those things? Maybe not. But I think I do."

Abigail returned his smile. "She sounds like a wonderful person."

"She was. But she was also very vulnerable. I never knew my dad. He left when I was a few months old. After that, my mom dipped in and out of relationships with several deeply unsuitable men. I know that now because there were always social workers in our lives. Some of the 'uncles' she brought home weren't nice people."

"But she wouldn't have put you in danger, surely?" Her grip on his fingers tightened.

"Not intentionally. I'm certain of that. But she was very sweet and gullible. I imagine the guys she dated promised her the earth." His lips twisted into a sad smile. "It's a pattern I see a lot. Then, one night, she left me with a neighbor while she went out to a bar with a new man. She never came home."

"What happened?"

"There were plenty of witnesses, who all told the same story. They both got drunk. Another guy asked her to dance. She said 'yes' but the boyfriend objected. They started arguing and he swung a punch. My mom fell and hit her head on the corner of a table. The bar staff acted quickly but she was dead before the ambulance arrived."

She shifted in her seat so she was facing him. "What an awful thing for you to face as a child. Did you have any other biological family?"

"No. It had always been just the two of us. My mom had spent her own childhood in a series of foster homes—" He shrugged. "The irony is that she'd been determined to make sure I wouldn't go the same way."

"She couldn't have predicted what would happen." Abigail sounded almost fierce. "No one could. What about your father? Didn't he come forward when he knew your mom was dead?"

"My dad was forty-two when he met my mom. She was twenty. He was diagnosed with bipolar disorder, receiving a pension from the army following a breakdown during basic training twenty-six years earlier. When I was born, he had been addicted to alcohol and over-the-counter painkillers for most of his life," Griffin said. "He couldn't care for himself, let alone a child. When officials from the Michigan Department of Health and Human Services tracked him down, he told them he wanted nothing to do with me. Years later, I read my file. The caseworker in charge commented that, in the circumstances, no contact would be best for both of us."

Although he was able to look back now and feel empathy for the broken man who had fathered him, his memories of that time, in contrast to those from before his mother's death, were shrouded in murky terror. The nightmares, the tears, the need to see his mom again, and the ever-present "who will care for me now?" questions were as real to him today as they had been back then. Over time the feelings of abandonment and rejection had subsided, but they'd never gone away. He'd learned to understand that no one had been at fault. His mom had been struggling to do her best against the background of her own problems. Through no fault of his own, his dad had been unable to offer even the basic requirements of fatherhood. Even his mother's killer hadn't meant to cause her death.

There was no blame. Only fragments of broken lives. Through the years, Griffin had examined them, tried to understand, but never fully pieced them together to make sense of his life story. By the time he became a Colton, he was already his own person, destined to be forever in the middle of two lives.

"You must have needed so much help. Please tell me you were given the right kind of support," Abigail said.

"There were certainly people who wanted me to talk to them. But I'm not sure they understood what I needed." Griffin frowned as he tried to explain what he meant. "I was seven years old. I didn't want to talk about my feelings. I just wanted my mom."

"That's so sad." She reached for one of the paper napkins that had come with the takeout order and blew her nose. "It must have been the most awful time in your life."

He was amazed that, with everything that was going on in her own life, she could be moved by his story. Having been brought up from the age of seven in an empathetic family, he was used to people tuning into his feelings. This felt different. It was as if Abigail was so in tune with his emotions, she was absorbing some of the hurt he always carried with him. The thought was comforting and scary at the same time.

"What happened next?" Abigail asked.

"Graham Colton defended the guy who killed my mom." Griffin scooped up a forkful of noodles and ate them before continuing. "He was charged with murder, but Graham got the sentence reduced to assault."

"Oh." She blinked in surprise. "How did you feel about that?"

"At the time, I knew nothing about it. I was protected from what was happening. Now? I guess it was the right outcome. He was a jerk, but he didn't intend to kill her."

"I don't know if I could be as forgiving." The corners of her mouth turned down. "But you found a home with the Coltons?"

"Yes. Graham told Kathleen about the case, and she was moved by my story. They adopted me soon after."

Griffin had never encountered anyone with a gaze as a perceptive as Abigail's. It was as if those hazel eyes were probing his thoughts. "It must have been very hard to adjust to a new family so soon after losing your mom."

"It was." Although she was easy to talk to, he now found himself hitting the emotional equivalent of a brick wall. If he got started on what he'd lost and gained when he became part of a new family... Well, he just wasn't ready to go there. Instead, he held up one of the cartons. "Care to split the last spring roll?"

As they finished the meal, Griffin steered the conversation toward less personal topics, including a local news item about a spate of thefts from a bakery. Security footage had shown that the perpetrator was the owner's dog. Although she laughed at the story, Abigail remained shocked by what Griffin had told her about his early life.

Now, it appeared he had retreated behind a barrier as though he was afraid he'd revealed too much. She didn't want him to regret having confided in her, and she wanted to let him know how much she valued his trust in her.

Would it help if he knew they had something in common? She figured it was worth a try.

"The circumstances were different, but I lost my own mom when I was very young," she said.

"I know you said she left your dad."

"When I was ten. I never saw her again after that and she died in a car crash when I was thirteen."

"I'm sorry. I didn't know."

"Why would you?" Abigail managed a slight smile. "I'm guessing your research into my family has covered my father's business activities rather than our personal lives."

"You're right." His expression was somber. "But telling you about my own mom could have been triggering for you. I didn't consider that."

She shook her head. "That's not why I'm telling you this. You shared your story with me. I wanted to do the same."

"Why didn't you see your mother after she left? That's a very unusual situation."

"Looking back, I'm amazed she stayed with him as long as she did. I found out later that she tried to leave and take me with her on several occasions, but my dad stopped her each time. In the end, it all became too much. She sneaked out one night to a place where he couldn't find her. With the help of some friends, she started a fight for custody." She bent her head, studying the wood grain of the tabletop. "He used every cheap shot he could come up with to make sure she couldn't win and that we never got to see each other."

"If you never saw her again, how do you know all of this?" Griffin asked. "Did your dad tell you he used unfair tactics?"

"No, although he wouldn't see it as a bad thing. He takes pride in being good at fighting dirty. My mom wrote me a letter just before she died. Actually, it was one of many, but it was the only one I received. I don't know what happened to the others, but I guess my dad intercepted them. Somehow, this one got through."

Whenever she remembered that time, the confusion and grief she'd experienced resurfaced. Her dad had told her that her mom had gone because she no longer cared about them, and the absence of any contact had seemed to reinforce that. For a long time, Abigail had questioned her own role in the breakup. Had it been her fault? Had she somehow caused her mother to fall out of love with her dad? With her? Feeling unloved and rejected, she had withdrawn into herself.

"Do you want to talk about what it said?" Griffin asked.

She reached for another napkin and dabbed at the corners of her eyes before blowing her nose again. Such a good look. Was this what he'd expected when he offered to come over? But he was such a good listener, and they'd established an almost instant bond through their similar backgrounds. For the first time since Veronica's death, she didn't feel embarrassed about showing her feelings in front of another person.

"Mom wrote how much she loved me and how hard

it had been to leave. In the end, my dad had made her life such hell that she'd had no choice. His wild business schemes, debts and dubious acquaintances were taking over his life and, at the same time, his controlling behavior toward her was increasing. He wouldn't allow her to leave the house without him and wouldn't give her any money of her own. In that letter, she told me how hard she'd tried to get custody and to have contact with me." She managed a laugh. "The thing is, my dad never really cared for me that much. Keeping us apart would have been driven more by the desire to hurt my mom than any love he felt for me."

"I'm sure he cared for you in his own way." His voice was gentle.

"Are you?" she asked. "Think about what you know of the RevitaYou scam. Do you think the man behind that sounds like he would be a loving parent? And yet, his own mom was loving and kind. I grew up close to her, even though my dad wasn't a family man. She died of Alzheimer's and that prompted my interest in the disease."

"Yet, even despite your mom's letter, you didn't get to see her before she died?"

"The letter made things worse. I tried confronting my dad but he refused to listen when I asked to see my mom. When we got the news that she was dead—" She tilted her head back and looked up at the ceiling for a moment or two. "The first thing he said was that at least I would finally stop annoying him about contacting her."

Although Griffin didn't comment, his fist clenched

on the tabletop. After a few moments, he pointed at her empty beer bottle. "Another?"

"Thank you, but two is my limit. Maya will wake me up at about six tomorrow morning, so I need a clear head."

"Did you go to your mom's funeral?" he asked.

"Yes, even though my dad told me I couldn't. Veronica and I sneaked out of school that day and went to the service. I'm glad I got a chance to say good-bye."

"You should have been able to do so much more." His voice was gruff. "Too many people are inclined to view divorce as just another episode in a child's life. It's not. It's a major trauma that changes the whole trajectory of a person's future. In your case, you had so much else to deal with in addition to your parents splitting up."

She smiled at him. "You are the most amazing advocate for children."

"I do my best."

When he smiled, she realized that she'd been mistaken. He wasn't cold. He was shy.

"When Riley checked on your dad's background, he discovered that Wes was an investment banker." Griffin changed the subject.

"That's one of the jobs he had," Abigail said. "He used to be good with money, but then his age became an issue for the firm he was at. He started complaining about younger people being given all the opportunities. He was always a scammer and what he meant was that he was missing out on the chance to make more cash. He said he was leaving to start a new venture. He was a grifter and I guess RevitaYou and the pyramid scheme was his latest plan. I feel so bad for all the people who got taken in and lost money."

"It's not just about money. The reason we started to investigate this con is because of a man called Brody Higgins. My dad got involved in Brody's case when he was wrongly accused of murder. Since then, we've all looked out for Brody—he's like part of the family. Brody borrowed five thousand dollars from a loan shark company called Capital X to get in on RevitaYou. When he didn't meet the first payment, they broke two of his fingers. Now he's on the run trying to avoid the next attack."

"That must be so worrying for you and your family," Abigail said.

"More for them than for me. Brody might have been another late addition to the family but he was a very important one."

There was something about Griffin's expression as he spoke that drew her attention. She sensed there was a tension in him about how the Coltons treated Brody. Clearly, his past was complicated and still affected him today. Yet he had turned all that hurt into a powerful force for good. She knew about the amazing work he did for children, not just in his job, but for nonprofit organizations in the Grand Rapids area. It told her so much about the sort of man he was that he could empathize so strongly with children in the foster and adoption system and he would devote his life to helping them.

"I should go." He indicated the clock over the stove.

"Goodness, how did it get to be after midnight?"

He laughed. "I'd love to stay and talk some more but I have an early start. And you did say you'll be woken at six."

She walked with him to the front door. He paused and faced her in the confined space of the hall. As he raised his arms, she thought he was going to pull her in close for a kiss. Her heart started to beat a little faster and she held her breath. He hesitated for a second, then rested his hands lightly on her shoulders.

"I enjoyed tonight, even though the circumstances weren't ideal."

She nodded. "And some of the topics we talked about weren't exactly uplifting."

"But it was good to be able to share those difficult parts of our lives." He moved his hands down to her upper arms, warming her flesh through the thin material of her shirt. "Let me know if you hear any more about the Anthrosync investigation. I'll keep you informed if I get any information from your caseworker."

When he'd gone, Abigail locked the door and slid her hands down her arms, touching the place where his fingers had just rested. Surely it was wrong to feel happy when her life was falling apart so spectacularly?

Wrong or not, being with Griffin made her feel good and she was glad of his protective presence in her life. And the fact that she found him so attractive?

Well that was a complication she would have to deal with. *How* she would deal with it, though—that was something she hadn't quite figured out yet.

Chapter 5

That night, Abigail surprised herself by actually sleeping for a few hours. In addition, Maya slept past her usual time the following morning. As a result, the baby woke with a raging appetite and immediately demanded food. For someone who couldn't yet talk, she sure knew how to voice her requirements. After strapping her into the high chair, Abigail was preparing oatmeal and pouring milk into a sippy cup, when the doorbell rang.

Frowning, she went to answer it. It was still before eight. She had called the daycare to let them know they were running late but she had no idea who could be calling at that time, particularly as she would usually be heading out about now.

When she opened the door, the tall man standing on the doorstep had an air of authority that was reinforced when he held up his police badge. "Dr. Matthews?"

"Yes." The sinking feeling in the pit of her stomach was intensifying with each passing second.

"I'm Detective Emmanuel Iglesias of the Grand Rapids PD. May I come in?"

A wail from the direction of the kitchen signaled that Maya was growing impatient. Although Abigail would have liked to find out more about why there was a police officer at her door *before* she asked him in, she wasn't prepared to keep her daughter waiting any longer.

"I need to feed my baby while we talk." She stood to one side to allow the detective to step inside.

As she led him through to the kitchen, her imagination was going wild. Had they found her dad? Had he somehow implicated her in the RevitaYou con? Had he committed another crime? Or had the Anthrosyne investigation become a criminal inquiry? There were so many things going on in her life and she just couldn't imagine any good reason why a detective would be knocking on her door at eight in the morning.

The blood in her veins seemed to have been replaced with ice water and, when she went to take the oatmeal out of the microwave, her hand shook.

"It's okay, honey." She forced herself to sound normal for Maya's sake. "Breakfast is coming right up." She turned to Detective Iglesias. "Can I get you anything? Coffee, maybe?"

He shook his head. "I can see you're busy, so I'll get straight to the point. I'm investigating the murder of Dr. Evan Hardin."

Abigail had been about to stir the oatmeal but, at those words, the spoon slipped from her fingers and clattered to the floor. "What?"

She must have misheard. Things like murder inquiries belonged on TV and in the movies. They didn't happen in real life.

"Dr. Hardin was found dead in his office this morning. The time of death is still to be confirmed but we believe it was sometime yesterday evening."

Mechanically, Abigail picked up the spoon from the floor and placed it in the sink. After getting a clean one from the drawer, she went to sit beside the high chair. Maya babbled happily and opened her mouth like a baby bird. A rush of nausea washed over Abigail and she bowed her head until it passed.

"You said he was murdered?" Images flitted through her mind of the kind, serious man who had been her supervisor and friend throughout her time at Danvers University. Why would anyone kill Evan Hardin? He was an academic. The sweetest, most inoffensive man she'd ever met.

"He was hit over the head from behind with a blunt object. A blood-stained glass bowl, from his awards shelf, was lying next to the body. I'm in the initial stages of my inquiry but it appears that it was the murder weapon. Nothing appears to have been taken." He took a small notepad and pen out of his shirt pocket. "I believe Dr. Hardin was your boss?"

"Wait." Abigail looked away from Maya's oatmeal covered face. "Am I a suspect?"

"All I'm doing right now is making some preliminary inquiries." He was close enough for her to see that he had written the date and time next to her name at the top of a blank page. "But I've been given information that you and Dr. Hardin had an argument yesterday. Something to do with your suspension from your job because of your use of illegal substances?"

Her situation was bad enough, but what he'd just said made it sound so much worse. And, if Evan's body had been found only that morning, who had given the police false information about her? Was it the same person who had provided details of the use of Anthrosyne in the Mem10 trial? Either way, Abigail felt under pressure. She had no way of defending herself against an invisible threat and yet it felt like the evidence was stacking up against her. The *nonexistent* evidence.

"I want to speak to my attorney before I answer any questions." If that made her sound guilty, she didn't care. Because of RevitaYou, the rest of the world already viewed her that way. From now on, she was putting herself, and Maya, first.

"You have that right, of course."

There was just one problem. Abigail didn't have a lawyer. At least, not one who specialized in criminal law. What she had was an adoption attorney. But she trusted Griffin. Because of the connection that had sprung up between them, she knew he would support her better than anyone.

She spooned the last of the oatmeal into Maya's mouth. "I need some privacy while I make a call."

He rubbed a hand over his chin and gave her a weary look. "I could come back later."

"Thank you." She wasn't going to let him make her feel guilty about taking control. Even after a reasonable night's sleep, she was tired and stressed. Her future with Maya was too important to risk on a wrong word to a detective. "I'll have my attorney call you to arrange a convenient time."

When he'd gone, Abigail leaned against the wall for a moment or two. Her knees were trembling, and she wanted to cry. But she didn't have time to be upset.

Please let Griffin answer...

With fingers that shook slightly, she found his number in her cell phone and swiped to make the call. It went straight to voice mail.

Choking back the sob that rose in her throat, she forced herself to speak calmly. "Please call me back as soon as you get this message. It's important."

For now, that was all she could do. Maya needed normality, and that was what Abigail would give her. Pinning on a smile, she returned to the kitchen.

"Hey there. How would you like to go for a walk in the park?"

Maya showed her appreciation of the idea by hammering her spoon on the tray of her high chair before throwing her sippy cup on the floor.

Her stress levels were off the scale, but she was a mom and Maya's care was at the top of her list of priorities. As she focused on packing a bag with the baby's essentials, she found her breathing slowly returning to normal.

Staying in control. For now, it was all she could do. And for Maya's sake, she would do it the best way she knew how.

"I'm not sure I can help you." Griffin hated saying those words, but the couple sitting opposite him had brought him a case that was outside of his experience. "I think you need to take this to the police."

"That's what I said." Liam Desmond placed an arm around his wife's shoulders.

"But—" Shelby Desmond pressed a tissue against her lips before continuing. "We don't want to press charges. We just want our baby. Isn't that what you do? You bring families together?"

The Desmonds had come to Griffin in desperation when the private adoption they'd arranged had gone wrong. A woman on social media who said she knew about their fertility problems had approached them. After striking up a conversation via social media, the woman, who called herself Dr. Anne Jay, had explained that she ran MorningStar Families, an online adoption agency.

Liam and Shelby were desperate for a child of their own, but the waiting list was a long one and they had agreed to adopt the baby of a young woman called Kitty. They had sent regular payments to Dr. Jay who, in return, had obligingly sent them photographic evidence of Kitty's pregnancy and medical records. On the day the baby was due, they had transferred ten thousand dollars to MorningStar Families' bank account. Immediately afterward, Dr. Jay had stopped communicating with them on social media. They had no other way of contacting her. Griffin had spent some time looking into the online agency, but had been unable to find any contact details.

"To be honest, I would be surprised if there ever was a baby." Although Griffin spoke gently, he wanted them to know the truth right from the start.

Shelby covered her face with her hands and began to weep quietly. Her husband regarded Griffin with a mixture of annoyance and helplessness. "You think this woman could have done this before?"

"It's possible. Like I said, you need to talk to the police."

He didn't add that the arrangement the Desmonds had made with MorningStar Families was a questionable one and the chances of them getting their money back weren't high. The police should still be informed about the online adoption scam so that they could try to prevent it from happening again.

"Since you work with families all the time, maybe you could help to warn other people against this sort of thing?" Liam asked.

"I'll certainly try," Griffin said.

"If we send you some details, would you share them publicly?"

"Send them and I'll see what I can do." He would check with Pippa before making any promises, but he couldn't see what harm there would be in adding a paragraph to his monthly newsletter warning his followers to be aware that this sort of con existed.

When the Desmonds had gone, he checked the time. He had half an hour before his next meeting. Luckily that was routine and required no preparation. A regular lunchtime get-together with some of his fellow family law attorneys, at which they discussed their workload and difficult cases.

He just had time to check his messages. As soon as he picked up his cell phone, he frowned. Abigail had called him almost four hours earlier. As he listened to her message, he grew even more concerned.

When he called her back, she answered immediately. "Oh, thank goodness."

"Is something wrong?"

"My boss has been murdered." Her voice wobbled. "And I think I'm a suspect."

"Have the police said that?" He was reaching for his jacket and car keys as he spoke.

"No, but the detective who came around here made a comment about how Evan and I had a bad relationship. I told him I wasn't prepared to speak to him until I'd consulted my attorney." He heard her indrawn breath. "All I could think of was that I needed to call you."

"That was the right thing to do. I'm on my way over."

Before he left the building, Griffin arranged for his receptionist, Martha, to call his colleagues at the forthcoming meeting and offer his apologies. As he headed out to his car, he called Riley.

"Dr. Evan Hardin of Danvers University has been murdered."

"What? Isn't he Abigail Matthews's boss?" Riley sounded as shocked as Griffin felt. "What the hell is going on?"

"That's where I hope you can help me out. I don't have any information. Can you check the news channels, websites and social media to see what you can find out, then get back to me?"

"Leave it with me."

Griffin ended the call as he reached his vehicle. Riley's question was a perfect summary of his own thoughts. What the hell *was* going on? Could Abigail have killed her boss? His brain refused to process that possibility. As an attorney, he should be able to keep an open mind. As a man…? No, unless he was presented with undeniable proof, he wasn't going there.

When he arrived at Abigail's house, he was pleased to see her looking pale but calm. They went through to the den, where Maya was playing on the rug with a stack of colored wooden blocks. When she saw Griffin, she waved an aimless hand, but returned to her game.

"Don't be fooled into thinking she'll stay there," Abigail said. "She doesn't crawl, but she wriggles on her stomach. If I look away, she can be across the room in seconds."

"She's gorgeous." They watched the little girl together for a few seconds. "You are very lucky to have each other."

She nodded. "And I intend to keep it that way."

Although he was glad to see her fighting spirit was intact, Griffin noticed the tightness in her jaw muscles. He wanted to take that tension away.

"Tell me what happened."

"A detective from the GRPD came to see me just before eight o'clock this morning. He told me that Evan—Dr. Hardin—had been murdered. He was found in his office early this morning but they think he was killed yesterday evening. The police officer, a Detective Iglesias, said he'd been given information that Evan and I had a bad argument. That was when I told him that I wanted to speak to my attorney before I answered any questions."

"I know Emmanuel Iglesias," Griffin said. "He can be trusted to conduct a fair inquiry."

"But someone has already influenced his judgment of me," Abigail pointed out. "The way he spoke made it sound like he'd been told I was guilty of personally using a banned substance."

"Then we need to make sure he is given the facts instead of hearsay. Although—" Griffin frowned as a thought occurred to him. "If Evan's body was only found this morning, and Detective Iglesias was here by eight o'clock, the person who talked to him about you must have done it very quickly."

"What do you mean exactly?" Abigail asked.

"Think about it. I'm not sure how early your building is opened, but presumably the body was found by a cleaner or maintenance worker. That person would have called the police. A crime scene investigation team would then have arrived at Evan's office and

Emmanuel Iglesias must have joined them as soon as he could. It gives a very short time frame for someone to contact him with information about you. How did anyone even know that Evan was dead?"

"You're right. Unless it was someone in the building," Abigail suggested. "Scientific research isn't a nine-to-five job, so people are around early in the morning. If anyone saw the activity in Evan's office and found out what was going on, they could have approached Detective Iglesias with information."

"But why were they in such a hurry? The police will question everyone in time." Griffin stooped to pick up some of Maya's blocks that were beyond her reach. As soon as he handed them to her, the baby threw them away again. "No, someone was very keen to get your name out there from the start. They wanted the police to see you as a suspect even before the investigation started."

She appeared lost in thought for a few seconds. "Do you think that person was trying to frame me?"

"I do. And we have to consider that it could be the same person who introduced the illegal compound into your research program in order to sabotage your career."

"But surely—" She lifted a hand to her throat. "How far would a person go to make me look bad?"

"Were you going to say that no one would have killed Evan Hardin in order to place the blame on you?" She nodded. "I'm not so sure."

Abigail sat down abruptly on one of the two small sofas. "This can't be happening." The color had drained from her cheeks and she raised scared eyes to his face. "How could anyone hate me *that* much?"

Griffin went to sit next to her. Placing an arm around her shoulders, he drew her close and she immediately nestled against his side.

"You have to remember that this is not about anything you've done wrong. The reason behind what's going on here could be something you are completely unaware of. Until we know the identity of the person behind this, we won't know why they're focusing on you. Can you think of anyone who would do this?"

"I don't think I'm going to win any popularity contests right now. There are plenty of people out there who wouldn't rush to help me up if I fell in the street. But this?" She shook her head. "Tampering with a drug trial is bad enough. Killing my boss to make me look bad? I can't even begin to comprehend that."

"You said you'd been threatened by a former participant?"

She lifted her head, appearing momentarily confused. "Ryan Thorne? He's the son of a former Mem10 trial participant. Ryan withdrew his dad from the program when news about RevitaYou broke. He confronted me in the university parking lot yesterday before I met with Evan."

"What did he say exactly?" Griffin asked.

"He repeated the usual allegations about my involvement in RevitaYou. He's said in the past that there's no way I'm not part of it and how I'm the worst doctor in the world for creating such a terrible drug. Then he said he'd spoken with some other families who had withdrawn participants from the program. He said I'd get what was coming."

"Those were his exact words?"

She nodded. "I thought he meant I'd lose my job, or maybe be prosecuted."

"How many people withdrew from the Mem10 trial when they heard about RevitaYou?"

"Five." She bit her lip. "We started with fifteen people involved in the trial. But after your family started putting out social media blasts about the dangers of RevitaYou, a third left the program."

"I'm sorry. We didn't foresee the impact it would have on the work you were doing at Danvers University."

"How could you? And you needed a way to get the word out fast so that people stopped taking those dangerous vitamins," Abigail said. "I'm glad you acted quickly. I hope I'm wrong, but RevitaYou could prove even deadlier than anyone expected. Do you really believe that Ryan Thorne's threats could be connected to Evan's murder?"

"Believe me, having grown up in the Colton household, and doing what I do, my eyes have been opened to the best and worst of what people are capable of. And sometimes the most unlikely things can trigger a disproportionate and unpredictable response." Privately, Griffin could picture several situations in which an irate relative of a participant might turn his, or her, anger against Abigail's boss. Possibly Dr. Hardin had refused to discuss the Anthrosyne investigation, or listen to a complaint against Abigail, and the situation had gotten out of hand. He didn't want to distress her further by speculating. "I want to find out who was so eager to talk to the police immediately after the murder. If it was Ryan Thorne, or someone else whose relative is involved, they have some explaining to do."

Abigail was still nervous when Detective Iglesias returned. But with Griffin at her side she felt stronger and more prepared to face him.

"Griffin." The police officer nodded as he took a seat in the kitchen. Since Maya was sleeping in the den, Abigail had switched the baby monitor on. Now and then, faint sounds of snoring reached them. "Riley has already been in touch, but I told him I don't have much information about this case."

"Who else have you interviewed?" Griffin asked, as the three of them sat at the table.

"Dr. Matthews is the first person I've spoken to in connection with this murder." There was a definite change in the detective's manner. With Griffin he seemed slightly defensive, as though conscious that he would be required to explain his actions.

"And what are your reasons for questioning her first? We know she wasn't the last person to see Dr. Hardin alive," Griffin pointed out. "Dr. Jenna Avery entered his office immediately after Abigail. And, since that was early yesterday morning, it seems unlikely that he didn't speak to anyone else during the course of the day."

Emmanuel rubbed his nose thoughtfully. "Look,

I'm not making any judgments here. But I was told that Dr. Matthews and Dr. Hardin didn't have a good relationship after a recent incident. I wouldn't be doing my job if I didn't check that out."

"Ah, yes." As Griffin spoke, Abigail was seeing a different side to his character. She could picture him in a courtroom, tearing holes in the opposing side's argument. "The information you received straight after the doctor was killed. Who told you about that?"

Emmanuel looked surprised. "It was a message that was left for me at the university reception desk. I don't know who it was from."

"And you're happy to act on an anonymous note?" Griffin shot back angrily. "Is that how the GRPD operates these days?"

"Hey." Emmanuel was clearly riled. "I told you I wasn't reaching any conclusions here. This is a starting point. That's all."

"It's okay." Before Griffin could continue, Abigail placed a hand on his arm. "I'll explain the situation to Detective Iglesias. I have plenty of emails from Evan to back up my story. They show that our relationship was a good one."

"Okay." Griffin's expression lightened slightly, but, as he looked at Emmanuel, she could tell he still wasn't happy. "But I want you to do everything you can to find out who sent that note."

The detective held up his hands. "I'll try but it won't be easy."

"Then I want it on the record that my client is

freely helping the police despite being questioned on the strength of one very dubious piece of evidence."

"Your client?" Emmanuel raised an eyebrow. "You're practicing criminal law now?" Griffin gave him a frosty look. "Okay. I get the message. Attempts at humor will not be appreciated."

"Dr. Hardin and I did not have a difficult relationship," Abigail said. "On the contrary, we had worked well together for a number of years. I am in charge of one of Evan's research programs. It's a series of clinical trials to test efficacy of a new memory boosting over-the-counter supplement called Mem10. My paternal grandmother died from complications from Alzheimer's and this field has always been dear to my heart."

She bowed her head. This was the hard part and she still couldn't believe she was having to explain this to anyone, let alone a police officer.

"I recently learned that my bid to adopt my foster daughter has been stalled. That was when I discovered I was being investigated over an allegation that I'd used an illegal enhancement compound, a designer, non-FDA-approved drug called Anthrosyne, to boost some of my participants' memories and to gain recognition for my work. The allegation was false, someone is trying to frame me. I have no idea who would do that, or why, but yesterday morning, Evan suspended me from my job pending an internal investigation."

"How did you feel about that?" Emmanuel asked.
"How do you think she felt?" Griffin snapped.

"How would you feel if you were suspended from the job you loved over something you didn't do?"

"I have to ask," Emmanuel said. "You know that."

Although he continued to scowl, Griffin held up his hands in a reluctant gesture of surrender.

"I was devastated but I understood Evan's position," Abigail said. "Neither of us would ever do anything to jeopardize the success of the program."

Emmanuel made a few notes before looking up. "What will happen to the Anthrosyne investigation now that Dr. Hardin is dead?"

"I don't understand." Abigail regarded him in confusion. "I expect another of the Danvers University leadership team members will take over. Why?"

"Just wondering." He tapped his pen on the table. "So the investigation doesn't go away because the guy leading it is dead?"

"Of course not."

"I think what Emmanuel is getting at is that, in terms of the Anthrosyne investigation, you had nothing to gain from killing your boss." For the first time, Griffin looked at the police officer with approval.

"I had nothing to gain in *any* terms." She wanted the words to be forceful, but her voice shook. "I am not a killer."

"Dr. Matthews, I am not suggesting that you are—"

Griffin cut across the detective's explanation. "Do you have a precise time of death?"

"The coroner has estimated that Dr. Hardin was killed between four and six yesterday evening. Until he completes his examination, we won't have anything more accurate," Emmanuel said. "He lived alone, so no one reported him missing. Unfortunately, his killer was in the building when he was working there. Why do you ask?"

"Just that Abigail was at Colton Investigations yesterday afternoon and I was here with her until after midnight last night. If her boss had been murdered around either of those times, I'd have been able to provide an alibi." As Griffin spoke, the doorbell rang. "Are you expecting anyone?" he asked Abigail.

"No." She shook her head.

Emmanuel checked his cell phone. "It's one of my colleagues. Some new evidence has come to light."

"Good," Griffin said. "The sooner you clear Abigail's name the better."

When Abigail went to the door, the second police officer introduced himself as Detective Daniel Lopez. He accompanied her into the kitchen and nodded briefly to Griffin before turning to Emmanuel. "We found something under Dr. Hardin's desk. It was missed in the initial search, but the CSI team recovered it when they conducted a more detailed examination of the murder scene."

He held up a plastic evidence bag containing a gold charm bracelet with the initials *A* and *M*.

"Is this yours, Dr. Matthews?" Emmanuel asked.

Abigail turned to look at Griffin, her eyes widening as the implications of what she was seeing hit her. "Yes. I lost it at work about a week ago."

Chapter 6

When the two detectives left, Griffin accompanied them to the door. "I don't want to tell you how to do your job—"

"Whenever anyone says those words, they always follow them up by telling us how to do our job." Emmanuel exchanged a weary look with his colleague.

"Don't you think it was odd that the bracelet was missed on the first search?"

Daniel Lopez bristled. "Are you implying that our CSI team didn't do their job properly?"

"No. I'm going one step further than that and suggesting that someone is trying to frame Abigail Matthews." Griffin fought to keep his anger under control. "She hasn't told you this, but she was threatened by the son of a former trial subject yesterday.

He told her she'd get what was coming. His name is Ryan Thorne."

"We'll check him out," Emmanuel said. "But, right now, Dr. Matthews still looks like our chief suspect."

"You don't have enough to charge her." Griffin was certain of that. An anonymous note and an item of jewelry that placed Abigail in Dr. Hardin's office at some point? Any decent defense lawyer would get the case thrown out within minutes.

"Not yet. When we do, we'll be back." It sounded a lot like a threat.

"Check the security footage in and around Dr. Hardin's office yesterday evening and this morning, if you haven't already." To hell with not telling them how to do their jobs. "Was Abigail Matthews in the Danvers University building? And find out if anyone went into his office after the first search and before the second one."

Neither detective replied but he could see them processing those instructions.

"Also, Abigail was at the CI headquarters with my family yesterday. My brother and sisters can vouch for that. She left in the middle of the time period during which you're suggesting Dr. Hardin was killed. If she crossed town to kill him, she'd have hit the rush hour traffic. When you have an exact time of death, you might want to check out the times to see if she could have done it within the time available. And, as I've said, I was with her and Maya at her house until after midnight."

Griffin watched the two men walk across the small

patch of lawn to their vehicles before he returned to the house. When he reached the kitchen, Abigail had her head in her hands and her slender shoulders were shaking.

Moving swiftly to her side, he drew her to her feet and held her tight against him. His intention had been to convey his belief in her and reassure her that he would be there for her during this fight. But, as he cradled her head to his chest with one hand and placed the other in the small of her back, a different feeling took hold.

With the warm softness of her breasts against his ribcage and his thighs pressed to her hips, the moment was magical and intimate. Ever since his mother's death, Griffin had believed that physical closeness was overrated. He loved his adopted family, but there had been a distance between them that he'd been unable to overcome. Holding Abigail was about more than wrapping his arms around her. He was enfolding her with his whole body, healing himself as well as her.

"I didn't do it." Her words were muffled by his shirt.

"You don't have to say that to me."

She looked up, her face streaked with tears and her eyelids red and swollen. "Thank you. You don't know what it means to have someone who believes in my innocence."

Her lips were close. So temptingly close that her breath brushed his lips when she spoke. Without thinking, he leaned in to kiss her. Gently, his mouth met hers. Taking all the time in the world, he softly explored the delicate curve of her lips. As she tilted her head to one side, he caressed the seam of her mouth with his tongue.

Winding her arms around his neck, she lightly nudged his tongue with her own. And passion ignited in an instant…but he knew he had to nip that in the bud. So… Griffin leaned back, examining Abigail's face. "Was that bad timing?"

"Possibly." She gave him a watered-down version of her usual smile. "But it was still very nice."

The doorbell rang and he felt a tremor run through her whole body. "You don't think it's the police again?"

"I'd be surprised if they came back so soon. Why don't I check it out while you make coffee?"

Although her expression didn't lighten, she headed toward the coffee machine on the counter while Griffin went to answer the door. The man who stood on the doorstep looked to be in his late twenties. His expression was serious, even slightly harassed, and he double-checked the front cover of the file he was holding when he saw Griffin.

"I'm looking for Dr. Abigail Matthews."

"Who are you?" The way the day had gone so far, Griffin was in no mood to waste time on politeness.

"My name is John Jones. I think we spoke on the phone recently, Mr. Colton?" Of course. This was the caseworker who oversaw Abigail's guardianship of Maya.

"I don't think Dr. Matthews is expecting you?"

"No. But I need to speak to her. It's urgent."

Griffin didn't like the sound of that, but he could hardly keep the guy standing there. Holding the door wide, he stepped to one side to allow Jones to enter. When they reached the kitchen, Abigail swung around to face them.

"John? Is everything okay?" It was clear from the strained look on her face that she didn't think it was.

"I'm sorry, Dr. Matthews. I've received information that you are a suspect in a murder case. In the circumstances, I have no choice. I have to remove Maya from your care."

I have received information...

Those words were suddenly dominating Abigail's life and she had no idea who was behind them. All she knew in that instant was that she couldn't let this man take Maya away from her.

"Please—" Sobs tightened her throat and she couldn't continue.

She couldn't see any way past the pain in her chest. The grief was too much. Then, from somewhere deep inside her came the will to fight. And that was what she needed. For Maya's sake, she would get past the hurt and keep going. "Abigail is not a suspect." Griffin's voice was calm. "As far as I'm aware, the police have no suspects."

The caseworker gave them both an apologetic look. "I've spoken to Detective Iglesias. He tells me that Dr. Matthews is under scrutiny for a number of reasons. Firstly, there is her father's connection to the

RevitaYou pyramid scheme. Then, of course, there is the Anthrosyne investigation and Dr. Matthews's suspension. Finally, we have the possibility that she may be implicated in Dr. Hardin's murder. And I believe there have also been threats issued against her as a result of some of these issues. Believe me, I wouldn't do this unless the situation was serious."

"But you can't think I would harm Maya," Abigail said. "And surely that's the only reason to take her from me?"

"You've been threatened, and that means that Maya could also be harmed…"

"Abigail has been Maya's only caregiver since her birth," Griffin interrupted. "And you must know that the baby is in no danger from her own foster mother."

"That's true. There is no question that Maya is in any danger from Dr. Matthews," John admitted. "But we have to consider Maya's overall welfare. The threats that have been made against you are too vague and could pose a danger to the baby. There are just too many negative elements for me to consider this a safe place for her."

"When will you be taking Maya?" Griffin asked.

"Right now."

"Oh, no." Jolted out of the shock that had kept her passive while they talked as though they were in a court of law and she wasn't there, Abigail made a move as if to block the door. Her thoughts broke free like a dam breaking. No one was taking her little girl. Not while she had breath in her body. "No."

She choked back a sob, terror gripping her. "This is her home. I'm her mom. You can't take her from me."

"I'm sorry." John looked uncomfortable.

"We both know Children's Protective Services is stretched to the limits and that includes the foster system," Griffin said. "Where will you take Maya?"

"I'll be honest with you, I don't know right now. We're so backlogged with cases that I don't have a clear plan. All I know is that Maya will have to be placed elsewhere until Dr. Matthews is fully cleared."

Abigail sank into one of the chairs, feeling the blood draining from her face. Clearly alarmed for her well-being, Griffin squatted at her side. "Breathe deeply. In through your nose and out through your mouth."

She gazed at him blankly. As she followed his instructions, the faintness that had threatened to overwhelm her gave way to a shard of pain in her gut. "My baby…"

She couldn't continue. All she could think was that she couldn't let this happen, but at the same time, her body was going into shock. Cold fear was spreading along her limbs and all she could do was stare at Griffin, as though searching for an answer in his eyes.

"*I'll* take Maya." He turned his head to look at the caseworker.

"Pardon?" John stared at him as though he'd just grown another head.

"I have been certified as a foster parent for five years. I keep my registration up-to-date and I'm known to your agency." He gripped Abigail's hands tightly. "What objection could there be?"

John gave him a doubtful look. "This is an unusual situation. I need to call my boss before I give you an answer." He gestured toward the hall. "Can I step outside?"

Abigail nodded. "Of course."

When the caseworker had left the room and closed the door, she picked up the still sleeping Maya and held her close, burying her face briefly in the little girl's hair, before studying Griffin's face. "I am not going to turn down this offer but what made you decide to become a foster parent?"

"Firstly, let me make it clear that, although I have certification, I have never actually fostered a child. I know very little about being a parent." He paused for a moment as if gathering his thoughts. "Being adopted shaped who I am, and not always in a good way. Don't get me wrong. I love my Colton family. I appreciate them and I am thankful every day that they are a part of my life. But I grew up feeling different from them. We don't share the same genes. I never had those bonding moments when you look at someone across the room and realize that you resemble them."

He shook his head as though wondering where this outpouring was coming from. She thought again about her first impressions of him as a stiff, unyielding figure and how wrong she'd been.

"In spite of that, what Graham and Kathleen did when they offered me a place in their family has always resonated with me. I am in awe of people like them." He lifted her hand to his lips briefly. "And like you. People who offer a loving home to a child who is not theirs by birth. If the time came when I was faced with a situation that needed me to step up, I wanted to be able to do it. But the paperwork to register as a foster parent can be time consuming."

She rolled her eyes. "Tell me about it."

"The agency screens the home and life of prospective foster parents, including family background, employment history, determination of any past abuse, criminal background checks, finances and medical history. They conduct a physical examination of the home, which includes cleanliness and condition, sanitation, fire safety and nature of the neighborhood in which the home is located. There is also a consideration of the desire and motivation to foster." Griffin ticked each item off on his fingers. "That sort of detail doesn't happen in a hurry. I decided that, if I was serious about being ready to step up at any time, I needed to have my certification in place and keep it up-to-date."

"And this is your time to step up?" Her voice was husky.

"I figure it's better than letting Maya go to a stranger or into a childcare facility."

She choked back a sob. "I don't know how to thank you."

"Hey." He used his thumb to wipe away a tear that trickled down her cheek. "You don't have to thank me. And there are some logistics we'll need to talk about—"

Before he could continue, John Jones came back into the room. "My boss has given his approval for you to foster Maya."

Griffin got to his feet. "I have a condition."

The caseworker and Abigail both regarded him warily. "I'm assuming that Maya will need to come and live in my home as part of the foster care plan?"

"That's right," John said.

"She's a nine-month-old baby who has only ever known the care of one person. Dr. Matthews is her mother. This is a very delicate stage in Maya's development. I am not prepared to do anything to unsettle her." He drew himself up to his full height, ensuring he had their full attention before making his next statement. "Which is why Dr. Matthews must move into my house with us until this matter is resolved."

Gratitude flooded through Abigail, leaving her speechless. This man, who she barely knew, was prepared to do this for her and Maya. He was going to turn his life upside down to make sure they could stay together. She already knew he was a good man. She was only just realizing that he was truly remarkable. Any woman would be lucky to have him as her partner and the father of her children.

"I'm not sure—" John tugged at his lower lip.

"What objection can there be?" Griffin asked. "I will be Maya's foster parent. I'll take full responsibility for her welfare and safety. And you've already admitted that she is in no danger from Dr. Matthews.

The perceived danger is from those who might wish to harm Dr. Matthews."

"But you work full-time," John said.

"I'll take a leave of absence. My junior colleagues can pick up my cases and I'll supervise them from home."

"In that case, I guess it will be okay," John conceded. "There will be some paperwork to go through."

"You can bring it around to my place." He turned to Abigail. "Does this arrangement suit you?" She nodded at him over Maya's head. "Right now, Abigail and I need to get started on packing Maya's stuff."

Almost immediately after John left, Maya woke up and started to wail.

"Since the child welfare authorities will do regular assessments going forward, I need to do some actual parenting." Griffin followed Abigail into the den and watched as she lifted the baby from the crib. "But I told you, I know nothing about this. I'm at a loss. Is she in pain?"

"No. She always wakes up hungry." The baby calmed down a little when she was cradled against Abigail's chest. "She has been eating solid food since she was six months old, but she still has formula several times a day. Although I keep it chilled, and there's no reason why she couldn't drink it at that temperature, she prefers it a little warmer."

As she spoke, she went back into the kitchen. Expertly holding Maya on one arm, she heated water on the stove, took a bottle of formula from the fridge, then poured the water into a jug and placed the formula into it.

"It only takes a minute or two." She smiled down at Maya as she spoke. "But this little lady doesn't do patience, so we have to sing songs while we wait."

Griffin regarded her in alarm. "I can't sing."

"Maya won't be judging your singing ability. It's the sound of your voice she's interested in." He thought he glimpsed a gleam of mischief in her eyes. "She likes rock ballads."

"You have got to be joking—"

"Quick. Or she'll start crying again."

He gave her a reproachful look and, from the depths of his memory, dredged up a song that his dad, Graham, used to play when he was driving. Fumbling his way through the first verse, he reached the chorus and was just starting to feel more confident when Maya, who had been regarding him with a horrified expression, threw back her head and started to scream.

"I told you I was no good at this," he told Abigail.

She made a suspicious choking sound. "I don't think she likes that particular band."

"In the future, make sure you give me her playlist in advance."

"Luckily, her formula is now ready." She retrieved the bottle from the jug of water and dried it with a muslin cloth. "You can redeem yourself by feeding her."

Maya had stopped crying, but she was still watching him with distrust. "Will she be okay with that?"

"As long as you have the magic bottle, she'll be fine." Abigail pointed to a chair. "Sit down and I'll hand her over."

Once Griffin was seated, Abigail placed Maya on his lap. Gripping her under her arms, he studied her with concern. She appeared to be quite robust. But how was he supposed to maneuver her so that he could get the bottle to her mouth?

"She's a baby, not a ticking bomb." There was a hint of sympathy in Abigail's smile.

Taking one of his hands, she drew it around Maya's body and eased the little girl back into the crook of his arms before holding out the bottle. The baby instantly grabbed it and pulled it to her mouth with a contented sigh. As she drank, her intent gaze fixed on his face and Griffin felt a new warmth bloom deep in his chest. This little person was somehow reaching out to him with that look, trying to figure out who he was, and establish a connection with him.

"Do you talk to her while she drinks?" Suddenly, getting it right was about more than food, and warmth and shelter.

"Yes. She likes that," Abigail said. "Don't worry about what you say. It's the sound of your voice that matters most."

She moved away and started to stack items of baby food together on the counter. After giving the matter some thought, Griffin decided to talk to Maya about a subject close to his heart.

"You may not know this, but there is a hockey team called the Grand Rapids Griffins. Their logo is a griffin. It's a legendary creature with the body, tail and back legs of a lion, and the head and wings of an eagle. You'd think it would be cool to be named after something like that, wouldn't you? And maybe it would be. For some people." Even though she had her back to him, he sensed Abigail was listening carefully. "Anyway, the Grand Rapids Griffins play at Van Andel Arena. We should go there during the season and you can help me cheer them on. You and your mom."

Maya drained the last of her formula and let out a loud belch.

"Not a hockey fan, huh? I guess if we can't enjoy the same sports, we can find out if we have other things in common. What do you like to do in your spare time?"

"She enjoys putting things in her mouth, especially things that shouldn't be there," Abigail said. "Cruising around the furniture is a new favorite, and she never tires of throwing things out of the bath, stroller or high chair."

"I guess I could learn to share her appreciation of those things."

"Right now, it's time for a diaper change." Abigail moved purposefully toward them. "And that's something Maya definitely isn't fond of."

"I'd forgotten about diapers." Griffin rolled his eyes.

"Get ready for your first lesson."

"I may have to ask my brother for some advice.

We have two sets of twins as siblings and he took on much of their care when we were growing up."

"He sounds like a good person to have on speed dial."

She took Maya from him and carried her through to the den. In a corner of the room, there was a changing mat and a plastic box with all the things that were needed for a diaper change. As soon as Abigail knelt and put Maya on her back on the mat, the baby giggled and rolled onto her front.

"You need to be fast." Abigail flipped her gently but deftly over again. Keeping one forearm across the little girl's stomach, she reached into the box and produced a toy that looked like a bunch of keys. When Maya saw it, she waved her chubby hands in the air until Abigail handed it over. She then alternated between shaking the keys wildly and chewing them. "And you need to distract her."

"Should I be taking notes?" He knelt beside Abigail, watching in fascination as she swiftly removed Maya's socks and pink sweatpants.

"Don't worry. I'll be right here at your side."

He wanted to tell her how much he liked the sound of that, although maybe not in the context of dirty diapers, but she was reaching into the box again.

"Talk me through what you're doing."

"I'm getting unscented baby wipes, so I can clean her skin. That's the best way to prevent diaper rash. If a rash does develop, she needs plenty of diaper-free time and some ointment to help her heal." Abigail placed the pack of wipes next to the mat. "We also need a biodegradable bag so we can dispose of the used diaper." She looked at him with a grin. "At least she hasn't pooped this time."

"How do you know?"

"Oh, you'll know when she's pooped." She leaned over to look Maya in the eye. "Go easy on Griffin. He has yet to encounter you at your stinkiest."

Maya chuckled and waved her toy keys in a celebratory gesture. It seemed to take Abigail only a few seconds to remove the old diaper, clean Maya's delicate skin and have her completely changed. Griffin was certain he would not be able to perform the same series of actions on the small, wriggling body so skillfully or quickly.

Once Maya was upright again and seated on the changing mat, she offered Griffin her toy. Touched by the gesture, he reached out to take it, only to have her snatch it away at the last minute. Still holding the keys, Maya clapped her hands and grinned at him.

"That's another thing she likes," Abigail told him, as she cleared away the changing accessories. "Playing teasing games." She sat back on her heels. "How will it work? Us moving into your place?"

"I have plenty of space. I grew up in Heritage Hill and always loved it. When it came to finding a home of my own, I knew there was only one place I wanted to live. Of course, those old houses aren't really suitable for a man on his own but I found a first floor apartment that needed renovation just a few blocks from the house where Riley still lives and from which he runs Colton Investigations."

"Those buildings are amazing." There was a genuine note of envy in Abigail's voice. "I remember walking around that neighborhood with my mom when I was very small. It was like stepping back in time."

"Trying to rebuild my place and stay true to the original style has been hard," Griffin said. "It's almost finished but it's been a labor of love. Anyway, I have three bedrooms, two bathrooms and a garden. There's plenty of room for Maya to play. There is just one thing I think we should talk about."

"What's that?"

"I think it's important to decide how we're going to introduce Maya to Lucy."

Chapter 7

The fact that Griffin had mentioned introducing Maya to someone called Lucy implied that this person was significant in his life. At that moment, Abigail realized she had made an assumption that he was single, based on the attraction between them. That, and the kiss they had shared. But she barely knew him. It was possible he was in a relationship and he cheated on his partner.

She wasn't comfortable with that image of him. No, it went deeper than that. She had started to develop feelings for him and she felt betrayed. Yet, it was at odds with her instincts and everything she had learned in the time she had known him. Griffin Colton was trustworthy when it came to his work. She *knew* that. But that left some unanswered questions about how he acted in his personal life.

She may as well start with the obvious one. "Is Lucy your roommate?"

He laughed. "That's one way of describing her." He drew out his cell phone and started scrolling. When he found what he was looking for, he held it up. "This is Lucy."

Abigail studied the picture on the screen. At least it wasn't a gorgeous woman. Instead, it was a cute creature with a pink nose, a circular blond stripe around its light brown face and teddy-bear ears. "Is it a kitten? No. A mongoose?"

"Lucy is a ferret. Full name Lucy Fur. As in Lucifer. Because she's a demon."

She cast a worried glance in Maya's direction. "When you say 'demon'—?"

"Oh, Lucy doesn't bite. She just steals things. And hides. And eats things she shouldn't. Like shoes and electrical cables." Griffin rolled his eyes. "There are some states that don't allow ferret ownership. I've told her I'm going to move to one, but Lucy doesn't respond to threats."

Abigail laughed. "What made you choose a ferret as a pet?"

"I didn't. Lucy chose me," Griffin said. "About two years ago, I found her in my garden. She was only a youngster and she was badly injured. I think she may have been in a fight with a cat or a dog. I took her to the vet, and they took care of her, but they had nowhere for her to go. Unlike cats and dogs, there are few animal rescue centers that welcome ferrets. I couldn't bear to see such a sweet, healthy animal euthanized, so Lucy came home with me."

"It sounds like she and Maya will get along just fine." She chewed her lip nervously. "But don't ferrets carry disease and bite?"

He looked relieved. "Lucy has a cage. It's not like she has the freedom of the house all the time. We can introduce them gradually and make sure they are always supervised."

She stooped to pick up Maya, feeling comforted by the baby's warm weight on her hip. "I don't want to disrupt your life, Griffin."

"Leaving my ferret in her cage for a little longer each day will not have an adverse effect on my well-being." He grinned. "Quite the opposite."

The temptation to return his smile was irresistible but she wanted to let him know she was serious. "You know that's not what I meant."

He placed a hand on her arm. "I want to do this for you, Abigail."

She studied his face, searching for something behind the smile. Growing up with Wes Matthews had made her suspicious of everyone's motives. With her dad there was always another angle, always a reason to turn on the charm. Although she knew there was such a thing as a nice guy, her judgment was skewed by her past experiences. Could Griffin be what he appeared? Strong, kind, dependable and protective? She hoped so, but she had learned to hold part of her trust back. Just in case.

"Why?" The word slipped out, and she winced. Would he think her ungrateful? Questioning his motives wasn't the best way to start this new relationship.

"Because I think you're innocent and you've had a raw deal. Because I want to make sure that Maya doesn't suffer because of what is going on." He took a step closer. "And because I like you."

Oh, goodness. The warmth in his eyes made her heart develop an extra little beat. Feeling like a schoolgirl with a crush, she gazed up at him. Clearly feeling that the moment had stretched out a little too long without any action, Maya reached out and gave Griffin a punch on the chin. The action broke the mood and, as they started to laugh, Maya clapped her hands.

"We should probably think about getting your things together ready to take to my place."

She sighed. "That's going to be such a big job."

"It doesn't have to be." He always managed to sound so reasonable and soothing. "It's not like you have to do it all at once. Pack enough for a day or two. We can always come back for more." He hesitated. "I don't want to pry, but are you going to be okay financially?"

"Yes. I have savings and a small legacy from my mom." She cleared her throat. "If you need me to pay rent..."

He looked horrified. "That was *not* why I asked. I was wondering if you needed a loan."

She started to laugh. "Are you always so sensible?"

"Do you mean boring?"

She shook her head, eager to reassure him. "That is the last word I would use to describe you."

"Maybe you can do some PR within my family? I could use some help to lose the reverse-rebel label," Griffin said. "Don't get me wrong. I don't want to be considered wild. But I've been the don't-know-how-to-party animal among my siblings for too long."

"If you're expecting me and Maya to change all that, you definitely don't know much about babies. I guarantee you'll be too exhausted to even think."

He laughed. "You're joking, right? How difficult can it be, taking care of one small child?"

At six o'clock the next morning, Griffin was seated at his own kitchen table. Uncertain whether he was dreaming, he gulped down a mouthful of coffee. It was hot and strong, the way he liked it, but his body was in shock after a sleepless night and he shuddered.

"Okay. I think the fact that my taste buds are working must mean I'm awake."

Abigail, who was slumped in a chair next to him, slowly turned her head in his direction. The movement seemed to require more effort than usual. "You took over pacing the floor with Maya from me. That was at two-thirty. She finally fell asleep at five. So, yes. Unless you've been sleepwalking all this time, you're awake."

Griffin rubbed a hand along his chin, feeling the stubble scratch his palm. "You said looking after a baby was exhausting, but last night was beyond anything I imagined. Is it always like this?"

"No." She sat up straighter. "Most of the time, Maya sleeps through. The only times she has a problem are if she's unwell, or teething. I think she had trouble settling last night because she's in a strange place."

"At least she's sleeping now," Griffin said. "I felt so sorry for her. And so helpless. It's awful seeing her get upset."

"You did a great job of comforting her," Abigail said. "It's distressing because babies don't know they're tired. They just know they feel bad. If Maya could just sleep, it would all be okay. But, of course, she cries and that makes her more exhausted and unhappy."

"I don't want the change of environment to have an adverse effect on her."

"She's resilient," Abigail said. "And, as you said, she has me to keep things normal for her. I'm sure she'll be okay." She smothered a yawn behind her hand. "Although we may be in for a few more sleepless nights before she gets into a routine."

Although she was pale, and her hair was mussed up, she still managed to look beautiful. Her pajama shorts and tank top showed off her long, tanned limbs and, even though he was so tired that lifting his coffee cup felt like a superhuman effort, her nearness was intoxicating. It was one of the things he hadn't thought through when he'd proposed this solution to her problems.

His first thought had been that Maya must not be placed with strangers. By offering to foster Abigail's daughter, he hadn't considered that mother and child would come as a package. Having them under his roof would bring him more challenges than he could have foreseen. And among them would be the attraction he felt for Abigail.

Or was he fooling himself? When he'd issued the invitation for Abigail to stay at his place with Maya, he'd realized that they would be in close proximity. Hadn't he been excited at the prospect and the opportunities it would bring? He was torn. Part of him wanted to take things further and act on the attraction between them. At the same time, he was conscious of her vulnerability.

Abigail was in danger. He was certain of that. Someone was trying to ruin her life and that person was so determined to succeed that he, or she, had already committed murder. Griffin was committed to protecting her and helping uncover the truth. Yet he was also part of the team working to find her father and bring him to justice. It would be stepping outside of his supportive role if he began a relationship with a woman in Abigail's position.

He had always taken such care to safeguard his heart. For the first time, he had an urge to set caution aside and see where his feelings might take him. The irony was that he couldn't act on it. He didn't know what the future held, but he'd have liked the chance to find out if Abigail had a part to play in his.

As Abigail tried to hide another yawn, he decided to focus on how he could provide practical help in the present. "Why don't you take a nap while the baby is asleep?"

"What about you?" Abigail asked. "We're equally tired."

"I need to check my emails and messages. I can always rest this afternoon."

"If you're sure?" She got to her feet. "Come and get me when Maya wakes up."

He placed a hand on his heart, pretending to be hurt. "Do you think I won't be able to cope?"

"I didn't mean—"

He laughed. "Get some sleep. Maya and I will be fine."

When Abigail opened her eyes a few hours later, she was confused by the light streaming through a gap in the drapes and by the strange room. Her first reaction was panic as she wondered why she was sleeping in the day and where Maya could be. As she came fully awake and recalled the events of the past few days, the initial alarm subsided. But the anxiety that had been with her since she had learned about the allegations against her remained.

She was still struggling to come to terms with how dramatically her life had changed. She had stepped outside her comfort zone when she'd agreed to adopt Maya but that had proved to be one of the best decisions of her life. Having lost Veronica, she not only had a permanent reminder of her friend in her life, she also now had a child of her own. The love she felt for Maya was as all-consuming as it had been unexpected at first.

But struggling with the loss of her closest friend, and still getting used to motherhood, she had then been hit with the shocking news about her father's role in the RevitaYou con. As a child, she'd been dazzled by him. His stories were magical. There was the pet monkey that played checkers with him. The time he smuggled diamonds out of South Africa. His heroic military record. As Abigail grew older, she began to see flaws in his anecdotes. Sometimes, the details changed...

She'd had other questions. Why did he have so many cell phones? Why did people call him by different names? Wes always had an explanation. Finally, just before her mom left, he had confessed. He was a spy, working at that time on a top-secret mission to foil a dangerous enemy plot against the government. Fascinated, and eager to see him in action, she'd followed him out of the house one afternoon. He'd gone to a local bar, gotten drunk and thrown up in the gutter on his way home.

And that was when it had hit her. Everything her father had told her about himself was a lie. Twenty-five years later, she wasn't surprised that he was still lying and cheating his way through life. What upset her most about RevitaYou was Wes's complete lack of concern for the consequences while he was taking people's money, often their life savings. Surely he must have foreseen that packaging a product that contained a poison and labeling it as a vitamin would cause harm to at least some of those who used it? The fact that he had gone ahead anyway was an indication that he didn't care.

What hurt almost as much was that so many people still believed that Abigail was part of the scheme. Ever since that day when she had realized that her father was a liar, she had been scared of her own genetics. Whenever she was faced with a tough decision, a little voice inside her head always wondered, "What would Wes do?" The answer was straightforward, of course. Wes would take the easy way, not the right way. So far, Abigail had been hand-on-heart happy with her own choices. She didn't take after her dad. Sadly, the rest of the world didn't know that.

Except for Griffin. She didn't know why he believed in her. She just knew he was genuine, and she was glad of his strength and encouragement when everyone else seemed determined to condemn her. His support had become doubly important since the Anthrosyne investigation and Dr. Hardin's murder. Without Griffin... She sat up abruptly. Fortunately, she had Griffin at her side. Picturing the loneliness and despair of fighting these allegations alone was a waste of time and emotion.

The apartment was very quiet. Too quiet for a place that contained Maya, who must be awake by now. Pushing back the bedclothes, she got to her feet. Still dressed in her shorts and tank, she slipped her feet into sneakers and pulled on a lightweight sweatshirt before leaving the bedroom. Following the central hall, she headed toward the kitchen.

There was a small closet to one side of the back door, and this housed the cage belonging to Lucy, the ferret. Although Griffin had shown his pet to Abigail and Maya on the previous day, Lucy had proved elusive, hiding in her bed with only the tips of her ears showing. Now, as Abigail passed, the little creature darted up to the bars and watched her with bright, beady eyes.

"Maybe we can hang out later," Abigail said. "Right now, I need to find my daughter."

It wasn't difficult to track Griffin and Maya down. All she needed to do was follow the trail of destruction. In the kitchen, there was cereal, milk and flour—*flour?*—on the floor. Going through to the den, she found most of Griffin's books pulled off the lower shelf of his bookcase and thrown onto the floor. Photograph frames were tipped over, cushions thrown from the chairs. Abigail recognized the hand at work. The scene looked like her own home most days.

She heard Maya's laugh and looked out the window. Griffin was sitting on the small lawn and the baby was wriggling on her stomach toward him. She appeared to be holding a plant.

Abigail retraced her steps through the kitchen and went out the back door. The yard was small and neat and the first thing she noticed was that a row of herbs had been pulled out of their pots and scattered across the steps.

"You should stop her when she goes into destructo-baby mode," she said.

Griffin greeted her with a smile. "Yeah. You'll have to show me how you do that. So far, nothing I've tried has had any impact."

When Maya saw Abigail, she dropped the leaves she'd been holding out to Griffin and raised her dirty hands to her mom instead.

"Come here, you." Abigail scooped her up and swung her round, causing Maya to squeal with delight.

She was conscious of Griffin watching them attentively. It was possible he was enjoying the moment or hoping to pick up some tips on how to deal with a nine-month-old whirlwind. But when she looked up and met his gaze, the heat in the depths of his eyes threatened to burn her up. It also ignited an answering flame deep inside her. A wave of emotion washed over her and she lost herself in that instant.

It was incredible that she could feel so attracted to him, in spite of the turmoil in her life. When she was with Griffin, she felt happy and at peace in a way she'd never experienced before. She only wished it was something they had time to explore.

"I saw that Maya trashed the kitchen. Did she happen to also eat breakfast?"

"Yes, she had cereal and a cup of milk. I wasn't sure how much to give her but, when she was finished, she threw the leftovers on the floor." He came closer and tickled Maya under the chin. "I sat her on the counter to clean her up and that's when she tipped a bag of flour over as well. She's fast."

"She is," Abigail agreed. "And stubborn. Once

she decides that she wants something, she doesn't give up."

"What about you? Did you sleep okay? Would you like some toast and coffee?" There was that smile again, the one that warmed her and made her shiver at the same time. "Although it's closer to lunch than breakfast now."

"I slept really well." She looked down at her unconventional outfit. "But maybe I should shower and change before I think about food?"

"You look great to me." As he spoke, he appeared to have second thoughts about the message his words might convey. "I mean, your clothes look fine." He paused, clearly thinking some more. "And so do you, of course."

Abigail laughed. "It's okay. Neither my clothes nor I need any further explanation of your meaning."

He rubbed a hand along his jaw. "I'm not used to this."

"Really? I'd never have guessed." They exchanged a teasing look that was lost when Maya rubbed a grubby hand down Abigail's cheek. "Why don't I take this little lady with me? That way we can both shower and change."

"While you do that, I'll make lunch," Griffin said. "And then I thought we could do some research into the scientist who assisted your dad on the RevitaYou scheme."

Abigail sighed. "I like part of that plan. And I guess we have to do the other part if we are going to move forward with the investigation."

Chapter 8

RevitaYou came in pretty green bottles, each containing a thirty-day supply of capsules. The accompanying glossy brochure was written in flowery language and promised to make the lucky purchaser look ten years younger within one week of directed use.

"Look." Griffin pointed to the very small print on the last page. "There are no contact details, but your dad is listed as the founder of the company. There is no information about who might have collaborated with him on this breakthrough invention."

They were seated side by side at the desk in his small office. Maya was taking a post-lunch nap and Abigail had brought the baby monitor into the room. The occasional mumble or snort reminded them of her presence.

Abigail leaned closer, her hair brushing his cheek as she squinted at the tiny writing. "I still have access to the forums on the university website. It's possible the project was mentioned when it was in its early stages."

Griffin shrugged. "We've done everything we can think of at CI. It has to be worth a try."

For the next half hour, they sat in silence while Abigail followed different threads and tried new searches. Just as she started to lean back in her chair with an expression of gloom, her gaze fixed on the screen.

"Landon Street. Ugh. I know that guy."

Griffin turned his head to look at her, trying to focus on the conversation instead of the fact that their faces were inches apart. "The way you said that makes me suspect that what you know of him isn't good."

"Landon Street has to be the most unethical chemist in the country. He worked at Danvers University a few years ago." The corners of her mouth turned down. "If there was a way to cut a corner, Landon would find it. He constantly skirted close to the edge of illegal practice. His research papers were sloppy, and he let his colleagues down time after time. I can't remember how many violations he had in the short time he worked at the university."

"What happened to him?"

"He took his shoddy methods a step too far. He'd already been moved into a lesser post because he couldn't be trusted. On the occasion in question, he was supposed to assist in a new clinical trial that would help elderly subjects with pressure sores. His supervisor gave him a schedule in which he needed to check each person weekly. Landon decided that was too often and, without consulting his boss, reduced the checks to once a month. The result was that one man developed an infection and almost died."

"That's criminal." Griffin was outraged.

"You're right, of course. The problem was that Landon's conduct reflected badly on Danvers University." She gave a helpless shrug. "It would not have been my way of dealing with the matter, but I believe the university settled out of court with the family and let Landon go but stopped short of suggesting his license should be revoked."

"That's appalling. He could have gone on to kill someone."

She pointed at the screen. "If I'm right, Landon could be responsible for formulating RevitaYou, and that may still happen. In this thread, there is a suggestion that he is working on a new vitamin."

Sensing her distress, he placed a hand on her wrist. "What happened to Landon after he left Danvers University?"

She frowned. "I don't know. Why do you ask?"

"I'm wondering how your father got to know him. Do crooked scientists advertise their credentials anywhere in particular? Maybe they offer their services to con artists through dedicated webpages or on social media?"

She managed a smile. "It's an interesting idea. But I'm not dodgy so I wouldn't know."

"I would never suggest that you were." He gripped her wrist a little tighter before opening his laptop. "Let's see what we can find out about Landon Street."

An internet search took them along a convoluted path. After leaving Danvers University, Landon Street's name cropped up in connection with a number of medical practices. It seemed he would lend his name to any venture, mainstream, alternative, even wacky. More recently, however, he had been involved in a few shady undertakings. There were beauty products, anti-aging drugs and miracle cures with his name attached to them. Quick fixes that had gone out of production within months, or even weeks, of their launch.

Scrolling through his history made depressing reading. If Wes Matthews had gone looking for an unethical scientist to assist him with RevitaYou, these credentials would have put Landon top of the list.

"Wait." Abigail was studying the search results with a puzzled expression. "Can you click on that link?"

It was an entry in article in a Danvers University online academic journal, written several years earlier. The writer had included a photograph of a team of scientists at Danvers University who had received an award for their pioneering work in researching prevention of early miscarriage. As she read it, Abigail leaned closer, the frown line between her eyes deepening.

"Is there a problem?" Griffin asked.

"Yes." Abigail pointed to the text on the screen. "This has been altered. See here, where the participants in the program are listed?" She pointed to a paragraph near the end of the article. "I was part of that research project and I know my name was included when this piece first went out. You can see from the photograph that I was among those who received the award. I'm right there, front and center. But all references to me have been removed."

Griffin whistled. "Why would anyone do that?"

"I don't know. To discredit me, maybe? But there's more. Landon Street is listed as one of the team who won the award. He didn't even work at Danvers at the time. He's not in this photograph."

Griffin followed the line of her finger as she pointed to the individuals on the podium holding up their awards. "How can you be so sure that the article has been altered and not that these were mistakes to the original?"

She scrolled down to the end, indicating the name of the author. "Because I wrote it."

An hour later, Abigail slumped back in her seat. "I don't believe this. We've checked five articles so far. Each of them included references to work I've done They have all been altered so that my name has been removed and another scientist has been inserted in my place."

"But a different person has been substituted each

time," Griffin said. "Only the first one gives credit for your work to Landon Street."

"Even so, it's like someone is trying to obliterate my achievements and ruin my career." She rubbed her eyes with her knuckles. "On top of everything else."

"Since we know he's crooked, let's start with Landon. Could he be the one who is behind the other attempts to discredit you? Even the murder of Dr. Hardin?" Griffin asked.

Abigail took a few moments to think about what he was asking. "Landon is not a nice guy, that much is clear from his actions. But is he capable of premeditated murder? I honestly couldn't answer that question because I don't know him well enough. And that's why I don't think he's the person behind the attempts to ruin me. He doesn't have a motive."

"He doesn't have a reason *that you know of*," Griffin said. "But if he has ties to your dad, who knows what's been going on behind the scenes? They could have fallen out and getting at you is Landon's way of paying Wes back. Or if Dr. Hardin antagonized him, Landon may have believed you were behind it, even though you weren't."

"Oh." She sprang to her feet, crossing her arms over her chest. "I wish we knew what was going on. This feeling that someone is out to get me without know who is just so frustrating."

He got up and came to her, placing strong hands on her shoulders. "And frightening. I know how scared you must be."

She rested her forehead against his chest. "I've

never known anything like this. The idea that I've made someone hate me so much—"

"Hey." He placed a hand beneath her chin, gently tilting her face until she was looking at him. "This is not about anything *you've* done."

She drew in a breath. "Try telling that to the person who killed my boss."

"Whoever murdered Dr. Hardin did it for reasons that were outside of your control, Abigail. The killer will try to justify it by blaming you, but you must never be drawn into that." He stroked her cheek with his thumb. "Stay strong. We'll get through this together."

Together. She liked the sound of that more than she could say. Rising onto the tips of her toes, she lightly touched her lips to his in a butterfly kiss. The gesture triggered a storm that nearly knocked her off her feet. Griffin's arms tightened around her, enfolding her in his embrace. He took hold of her chin with one hand, tilting her face up to his as he moved his lips over hers. This kiss was strong and warm, filled with passion, letting her know how much he wanted her. Instantly, her body ached for more. Arousal powered along her nerve endings, awakening a need within her, filling her with a passion that was unlike anything she'd ever experienced.

She clung to him, lost in the magic of his mouth caressing hers. He teased her, nibbling at her lower lip, flicking his tongue over the sensitive flesh. Sighing into his mouth, she surrendered to the delicious feelings churning through her. This was what it should feel like to be held by a man. She felt cherished and wanted. As though she had truly come to life at his touch.

Her lips parted, welcoming his tongue inside her mouth. She savored the velvet feel and warm, sweet taste of him. As their tongues danced and explored, he twisted his hands in the length of her hair. Finally, he broke the kiss and gazed down at her. The tenderness in his eyes said more than any words ever could.

"I think we forgot to be serious, dedicated investigators for a moment, there." She flashed a mischievous smile his way.

"Is that what we did?" His answering grin did something sinful to her insides.

Briefly, she rested her head against his shoulder. "Let's not get carried away. Maya will wake up soon."

He squeezed her upper arm. "Okay. Back to Landon Street."

Abigail groaned. "You sure know how to kill the mood."

He laughed. "You were the one who said we shouldn't get carried away."

"So it's my fault we go from delicious kisses to bad guy scientists?"

His eyes gleamed. "Delicious, huh?"

She bumped his shoulder with her own. "Oh, come on. You must have been told that dozens of times."

"Funnily enough, I haven't." His expression became serious. "Prior to getting involved in RevitaYou, Landon seems to have been lying low. Which makes me wonder where he is now. I need to call Riley."

"Do you want me to give you some privacy?"

He shook his head. "You're part of the CI team now."

As he got out his cell phone and found his brother's number, she studied the laptop screen, glad of a distraction. *Part of the CI team.* Apart from her job, she'd never felt part of anything. Even then, she'd always been the gecky girl on the fringes, rather than Miss Popularity. Coming soon after that incredible kiss, Griffin's words had caught her unawares and left her feeling shaken.

It was *him.* Griffin was the reason for her confusion. In the short time she had known him, he had turned her world upside down. His presence was reassuring and disturbing at the same time. And, while she loved the sensations this new attraction brought her way, she feared them as well. Until recently, her only meaningful relationship had been with her career. Now she was a new mom. She had responsibilities that were beyond anything she'd ever known before. Surely it was too soon to consider a romantic relationship as well? And with a Colton?

No. The hugs were wonderful. The kisses were even better. But she had to put them in context. Her life was in turmoil. She was scared, confused and lonely. Griffin had offered her shelter and protection, and he was the only person who appeared to believe in her. Was it any wonder she found herself drawn to him?

Try this attraction out another time. Like when life is back to normal. Whenever that might be...

"Riley? I need you to trace someone for me as part of the RevitaYou investigation." Griffin was talking to his brother. "A Dr. Landon Street. He's the person Wes Matthews used to develop the RevitaYou formula. I'm going to send you some links to his background but I also need to know where he is now. He may be able to help us find Wes."

He ended the call after chatting briefly to Riley about other matters.

"Do you think Landon could still be in touch with my dad?" Abigail asked. "They are in this together, after all."

"It's a possibility. The bad publicity following the social media blasts will have spooked them both. We know Wes is lying low, but there's a chance he and Landon have been in contact with each other. Maybe Landon even knows where Wes is hiding."

"It's like every piece of information we find about RevitaYou paints a worse picture." She shook her head. "And it was my dad who did this. He was the person who thought up this con. For the sake of the people whose lives have been affected, he has to face justice. But, and this sounds horribly selfish, I know that Maya and I will be tainted by what he's done."

"That's not true. When he's found, and the truth comes out, people will see that you had nothing to do with his schemes."

"But I'll always be Wes Matthews's daughter," she said. "And, even though Maya has never met him, she will always be his granddaughter. Assuming the adoption goes through."

"Maya will always be the daughter of the strong, beautiful woman who chose to raise her." His voice resonated with sincerity. "I wish there was something I could do to make this better for you."

"You do make it better, Griffin." In that moment her doubts faded to nothing. He hadn't come into her life at the wrong time. When she needed him, he was at her side. The future might bring its challenges, but that simple truth was enough for now. "Just by being here, you do."

Abigail was amazed at the way the Colton family worked so well as a unit. Griffin had told his siblings that they needed more of Abigail and Maya's belongings brought from home and the next thing she knew, there was a whole moving process underway.

The Coltons had packed up her place and delivered boxes and suitcases with clothes, toys and various baby items; unpacked; and put the contents away almost before she could tell it was happening. At the same time, with all the coming and going, Abigail was able to observe Griffin interact with his family.

It soon became clear that, in a group of big personalities, Griffin was the quietest of the siblings. Perhaps because he hadn't been born a Colton, he exhibited different traits and it showed most when the group was all together. While the others competed to talk, he remained reserved, cautious and introspective. His sisters, it seemed, were keen to let Abigail know the best ways to handle their strong, silent brother.

"He needs space," Sadie said, as she staggered through the door carrying a box of Maya's toys. "Give him time to think about things before expecting him to make a decision. He's self-conscious and he likes to consider options and consequences. If you're prepared to wait, he'll appreciate the lack of pressure and become more at ease with you."

"That's really helpful." Abigail helped her to carry the toys through to the den. "But you do know we're not in a relationship, don't you?"

"Oh, that." Sadie waved a hand in an airy gesture. "I just thought it would be useful advice."

"Yes." Kiely joined in the conversation. "I used to think that when Griffin was still and silent he was angry. Turns out, he's just recharging, or people watching."

Even in the midst of the lively family group, Abigail found herself watching Griffin more than any of the others. She wondered how someone so shy could be so successful in a career that required so much persuasive human interaction. And he was also able to switch on a forceful persona, such as when he dealt with her caseworker.

In the end, she was so fascinated by the contrast between his personal and professional personalities that she decided to ask him about it later that night when they were bathing Maya.

"Damn it. Just when I thought I was doing so well at disguising my introversion that you might actually believe I was outgoing."

"I just wondered," she explained. "You do such an

amazingly complex job, yet I don't think you enjoy being in a large group of people.

"You're right. Social situations don't come naturally to me. I don't do small talk and I prefer solitude to crowds. But my job requires me to mingle and to appear confident. So, over the years, I've developed a secondary personality. That's the person I become in social or work situations."

"That must be hard," Abigail said.

He shrugged. "It's second nature now."

As he leaned over the edge of the bath to splash water over Maya's upper body, the baby squealed with pleasure, making them both laugh.

Abigail sent him a sidelong glance. "Sadie was very keen to tell me how to handle your shyness."

He started to laugh. "I'll bet she was. My sisters are relentless matchmakers."

"Oh." She glanced his way again. "Have they been trying hard to find you a partner?"

"Why not come right out and say it? I'm thirty-two and still single. A hopeless case."

"What does that make me?" She held out a towel. Griffin handed Maya over and Abigail wrapped the baby up. "I'm thirty-five and not a man in sight."

"All I can say is that there must be something seriously wrong with the men of your acquaintance."

Embarrassed, she bent her head as she tended to Maya. "That doesn't sound like something an introvert would say."

"I don't feel very introverted when I'm with you." When she looked up again, he'd left the room.

* * *

"How can you be able to climb the furniture before you can walk?" Griffin lifted Maya down from the coffee table for the fifth time that evening. "I don't understand how that works."

While Abigail prepared dinner, he and Maya were spending some time together. Although he had decluttered the living room, he'd underestimated the baby's ability to get into mischief. Wriggling on her belly, she managed to get around the room pushing buttons, pulling wires, emptying bins and throwing, or chewing, anything she could find. As Griffin removed each item from her reach, she moved on to the next. Her own toys lay in a neglected pile on the rug.

At nine months old, she either didn't understand the word *no* or she'd developed selective hearing. Each time Griffin moved her away from a harmful item, she gave him an angelic smile and went straight back again. He knew babies were meant to be lively and inquisitive, but he hadn't been aware that their mission in life was to wear out the adults who cared for them.

He had a sudden flash of inspiration. "I know what you'd like. There is someone in this house who is even faster and nosier than you."

He'd taken Maya to look at Lucy in her cage a few times and the little girl and the ferret had regarded each other in fascination through the bars. So far, he had released Lucy only when Maya was asleep, taking the ferret for walks in the yard, or to climb in the park. Lucy was very tame and didn't mind wearing a leash and harness. As long as she could snuffle in the grass and under shrubs, or run up trees, she was happy.

Aware that ferrets had a reputation for nipping fingers, he didn't want to take any chances with his pet in close proximity to Maya. Probably because of her sad start in life, Lucy had the sweetest nature of any animal he'd ever known. She had never even scratched him, but a baby and a wild animal were a potentially volatile combination. With that in mind, he checked with Abigail. She was happy to leave the dinner cooking for a few minutes to help supervise the introductions.

"You're sure Lucy will be okay around Maya?" Abigail regarded the bright-eyed little animal with a combination of interest and caution.

"I'll keep Lucy in her harness," he promised, as he gently stroked the ferret's head. "I just thought Maya might like something else to do as a change from destroying electrical items."

"You could read her a book."

"Tried that." He rubbed his head reminiscently. "She hit me with it."

"There are educational games on my tablet." Although Abigail's expression was prim, her eyes danced with laughter.

"When she found out the tablet wasn't edible, she tried using it to hammer out a beat on the table. I think she may have a future as a drummer in a rock band." Maya, who had been looking from one to the other as they spoke, clapped her hands and bounced up and down on Abigail's knee. "See, she likes that idea. And I know a place where they can fix the screen on your tablet."

Abigail rolled her eyes. "Okay. Let's try the wildlife option."

After getting to his feet, Griffin placed Lucy on the floor. The ferret immediately scurried around, nose to the ground, her long body wiggling with pleasure. Holding the end of her leash, he followed her as she checked out every inch of the room. After a few minutes, having satisfied herself that there were no predators or rival ferrets lurking in any of the corners, she shimmied up the drapes.

Turning to look at Maya, Griffin saw that the baby was completely still, her eyes wide and her mouth open.

"All these books and lectures about parenting," he said, as he drew closer to Abigail. "And all that's really needed to keep a baby quiet is a small, furry creature on a leash."

She punched him lightly on the upper arm. "You do know that Maya will want to copy Lucy, don't you? From now on, she'll have a burning ambition to climb everything in the room."

This was what he'd been missing. Lighthearted exchanges and laughing over nothing. Little things that added up to big things. He wanted more of these moments with her.

Abigail's cell phone buzzed, and the moment was lost. She checked the number and frowned. "It's Dr.

Wallis Porter. He's a member of the Danvers University administration."

"Do you want me to take Maya out of the room?" he asked.

She shook her head. "I guess it will be about the Anthrosyne investigation and I'm fine with you hearing what they have to say." Her hand shook slightly as she swiped to answer the call, and he'd have given anything to have been able to take that nervousness away. "Dr. Abigail Matthews."

She listened intently for about a minute, her expression becoming more and more disbelieving. When she spoke again, her voice betrayed a combination of hurt and anger. "You must be mistaken. Dr. Jenna Avery is my subordinate. You can't appoint her to lead an internal investigation into my conduct."

It was clear to Griffin that Abigail was not convinced by any explanations she was hearing from the person on the other end of the call. Her cheeks flushed and her jaw tensed. After a moment or two, she cut in sharply. "I don't care how busy you are, Dr. Porter. You and I need to meet to discuss this. Tomorrow morning."

When she ended the call, she stared at Griffin, her eyes wide and scared. "What is going on?"

He used his free hand to grip her knee. "I don't know. Not yet. But we will find out."

Chapter 9

The next morning, while Abigail and Maya were still asleep, Griffin checked his emails. His colleagues had already dealt with most work-related items but there were a few things that needed his attention.

One of his messages was from Liam Desmond, the man who, with his wife Shelby, had been on the receiving end of the adoption scam. Griffin had been thorough in his research and Liam was thanking him for his work. Griffin scanned the items Liam had sent again. Not only were there copies of all social media interaction between the Desmonds and Dr. Anne Jay of MorningStar Families, he had also included any links he'd found to her and her online adoption agency. These were admittedly few, and vague.

Among the lengthy records that Liam had sent,

the only interesting thing Griffin had found was an old profile picture from one of Dr. Jay's dormant social media accounts. She'd been more careful recently to protect her identity, leaving no photographic trail, or other evidence that could be used to identify her. There was no guarantee that the woman in this picture was actually her. And, of course, the name Anne Jay was likely an alias, the title "Doctor" fake as well. Even so, it was a possible link, if the police ever tracked her down. Taken from the side, it wasn't particularly clear, but it showed she was young, possibly early thirties, white, and her hair was cut in a sleek, dark bob.

Griffin replied to Liam's email, reminding him again to contact the police and suggesting that the photograph might be helpful to them. He didn't point out that unless the police had a suspect, it was unlikely that they would be able to track down the perpetrator of the adoption con from a single picture. Ultimately, he believed that the Desmonds would have to accept that they had been the victims of a nasty fraud. Dr. Jay had probably moved on to her next target and a new scam. In all likelihood, she also had a new name.

"Coffee?" Abigail's voice from his office doorway provided a welcome distraction.

"Please." He studied her face. "You look tired."

"I didn't get much sleep," she admitted. "Maya has settled well after her bad first night. In fact she's still asleep now. But this new development in the Anthrosyne investigation is bothering me."

Griffin closed the lid of his laptop. "Let's go get

that coffee, then we can talk about the issues in more detail."

They went through to the kitchen and Abigail prepared their drinks. When they sat at the table, she cradled her cup in her hands as though trying to get warm.

"Tell me why you think putting this Dr. Avery in charge of the Anthrosyne investigation is another attempt to undermine you," Griffin said.

"Jenna Avery is one of my team on the Mem10 program and we worked together on the miscarriage project. She is a talented research scientist, but she's lazy. She cuts corners and doesn't complete paperwork to a good-enough standard. Until recently, I would have said she was also one of my friends at Danvers University. We used to eat lunch together, go out for dinner now and then—we'd meet up at the gym occasionally." When she looked up from her coffee cup, he could see the haunted look in her eyes, the one that usually meant she was thinking about her father. "That all changed one day in a team meeting. Without warning, Jenna started shouting abuse at me over RevitaYou. It turned out she'd bought a bottle of the tablets and got sick."

"Then she can't investigate you. Never mind that she's junior to you. She has a conflict of interest."

"I never thought of that." Abigail gave him a grateful look. "I wish you could come with me to this meeting. I'm so nervous I'm sure I'll mess it up."

He considered the matter for a moment. "If you want me there, I'll come. I'm your attorney. I know my specialism is adoption, but my role is to support you."

She started to lift her cup to her lips, but her hand shook so badly that she placed it back on the table. "Would you do that for me?"

"Of course. I'll admit I'm intrigued as to why the Danvers would appoint Dr. Avery to head the internal investigation. It sounds like she's not up to the job, but leaving that aside, it's not a smart move on their part since it leaves them open to allegations of incompetence or deliberately trying to get rid of you. Either way, I'm happy to help you fight back."

He was taken by surprise as Abigail leaned across the distance between them and wrapped her arms around him in a hug. It wasn't the most comfortable of positions, since she was on one chair and he was on another, but Griffin wasn't about to complain.

"Thank you." Her lips were pressed up against his neck and the sensation was maddeningly good. "There's just one thing we need to think about."

"What's that?" he asked.

She lifted her head, momentarily distracting him with the nearness of her mouth to his. "What will we do with Maya during this meeting? I've told daycare I'm on leave."

"If you're in agreement, we could ask Riley and Charlize to take care of her for an hour or two. It'll be good practice for when their own baby comes along."

"I don't know." She gave him a troubled look. "I've only ever left her at daycare."

He tightened his grip on her waist, enjoying the way she leaned closer. "You'd never introduced her to a ferret until yesterday. Now she has one as a new best friend."

"I'm not sure how your brother and his fiancée will feel about being compared to a small furry animal...and I don't want you to think that I don't trust your family."

"You don't have any reason to trust my family. But I hope you know that our investigation into your father's schemes would never affect our judgment where you or Maya are concerned."

"I'll admit I was worried that you and your siblings could have reached a decision about my guilt without knowing me," she said. "But now that I know you, I can see that you have higher standards than that." He could tell she was still fighting her natural caution where Maya was concerned. "If you're sure Riley and Charlize won't mind?"

"Once they get used to the exhaustion and know they have to hide anything that can be thrown or spilled, I'm sure they'll be delighted."

She started to protest, but he silenced her by pressing a kiss to the corner of her mouth. As he did, the baby monitor crackled into life with a series of demanding cries.

"Oh, that's something else I need to warn Riley and Charlize about." He flashed a grin at Abigail as she got to her feet. "Maya has perfect, or maybe I should call it *imperfect*, timing."

After leaving Maya with Riley and Charlize, Griffin drove them to the Danvers University adminis-

trative offices. Having observed her daughter closely
with Griffin's brother and his fiancée, Abigail felt reassured that Maya would be fine. Actually, she felt
slightly concerned that she would return to find her
daughter had taken charge of the household.

"She doesn't have to get her own way all the time,"
Abigail had told Charlize, as Maya was pointing to a
stack of pancakes on the kitchen counter while flut-
tering her eyelashes and making cooing sounds. "It's
fine to say no."

Since Riley had been gazing at the baby with a
besotted expression, and Charlize had already been
reaching for a bowl and spoon, she had little expectation of being listened to. It had always been at the
back of her mind that she and Maya had no family
except each other. Wes was their only close relative
and he had never shown any interest in his foster
granddaughter. He was hardly a conventional grand-
father and his recent behavior made his credentials
even less appealing. Uncle Riley and Aunt Charlize
were just what her daughter needed.

But she was getting a little ahead of herself. They
had stepped in to babysit as a one-off. It wasn't like
Griffin's family would be there for life. The thought
had caused her cheeks to burn. Distractions were not
what she needed. Not today.

As Griffin found a space in the parking lot, Abigail gazed at the familiar building. It had been her
workplace for the last five years, yet it felt hostile to
her now. The decision to appoint Jenna Avery was so
bizarre it felt like a declaration of intent. As Griffin

had said, it either meant her employers were incompetent, or that they intended to get rid of her. And she didn't believe the university administration was incapable of doing its job. Dr. Wallis Porter had headed up the human resources department for over twenty years and he was as sharp as a tack.

Which left her with a nasty reality. She was no longer welcome at Danvers University. Could she blame those in charge for reaching that decision? She was the daughter of the man behind a particularly nasty con. The publicity surrounding the dodgy vitamins hadn't impacted the university yet but it was only a matter of time and Abigail felt that the clock was ticking. They were on a countdown to the first Revita-You death...

The fallout had already been felt, though. Ryan Thorne might be the most vocal, but she knew that others had made complaints about her, asking how the university could continue to employ someone with her connections. It didn't matter that, in reality, her record was blemish free. All that counted was the perception.

Wes Matthews's daughter. Tainted by association.

Add the Anthrosyne allegation into the mix, and even before the investigation started, she was doomed.

"Why didn't I see that?" She spoke aloud without thinking.

"Pardon?" Griffin turned his head to look at her.

"I can't survive this, can I?" She bit her lower lip to stop it from trembling. "It doesn't matter who con-

ducts the Anthrosyne investigation, or what the outcome is. My reputation is ruined, both here at Danvers
University and as a research scientist."

"Once we clear your name, the damage will be un-
done," he said. "People have short memories. Before
long, they will move on to the next story."

She nodded. "I know you're right. It's just so hard
when we're in the middle of this one."

He pressed her hand. "Let's go get 'em."

They exited the car and crossed the parking lot.
The sensation that she was being watched from the
building made Abigail square her shoulders. She'd
done nothing wrong. She'd worked there happily for
so long. She wasn't about to enter the place now like
a condemned woman.

Once inside, she went to the desk. The receptionist looked up with a smile. "Oh, Dr. Matthews. Hi."

The friendly greeting made the situation seem
even more surreal. "Dr. Porter is expecting me."

The receptionist consulted her computer screen.
"Yes, he is. Please come with me."

The last time Abigail had been into this part of
the building, she had accompanied Evan Hardin to
his office. As she and Griffin followed the receptionist, the thought chilled her. Was there something she
could have done that day that would have changed
the outcome for Evan? Had anything she had said or
done contributed to his death? It was impossible to
believe that the man she'd known and cared about
was dead, that his murder could somehow be linked

to her. The thought jogged something in her memory. Something Evan had said...

When they reached Dr. Porter's office, the receptionist knocked before moving aside to let them enter. The administrator rose from his seat behind his desk when they stepped into the room. Although he was nearing retirement, he still had the air of a man who had occupied a position of authority for many years.

"Dr. Matthews." After nodding to Abigail, he turned to Griffin with an inquiring look.

"Mr. Colton is my attorney." A brief look of annoyance flashed across Dr. Porter's features and Abigail was glad. She wasn't here to make things easy for him.

"I'm not sure—"

"You're not sure if Abigail is entitled to representation at a meeting with her employer?" Griffin's tone was pleasant, but his manner reminded Abigail of a hawk about to swoop on its prey. "Why would you be in any doubt about that, Dr. Porter?"

"That's not what I meant." There was a hint of snappiness in the response and Dr. Porter waved them to two seats on the opposite side of his desk as he resumed his own seat. "I was simply unaware that this meeting required such formality."

"Clearly it does," Griffin said. "Since the person you have appointed to replace Dr. Hardin as the Anthrosyne investigation lead is not only junior to Abigail, she is also known to be antagonistic to her."

Dr. Porter frowned. "I'm not aware of any antagonism."

"Jenna Avery was publicly and recently confrontational to me," Abigail said. "She accused me of being involved in the RevitaYou con and blamed me for the fact that she had become ill after taking some of the vitamins. Her allegations were witnessed by at least twelve Danvers University staff."

"This raises a number of issues for you, as the head of Human Resources, at this university," Griffin said. "The first, of course, is the potential damage to Abigail's well-being from being subjected to such a distressing personal attack in her workplace." Griffin leaned forward slightly in his seat, ensuring he had the other man's full attention. "She prefers to hope that these accusations, whether they are from the families of participants, or whether they are anonymous, will die out over time. However, it was particularly upsetting to be confronted in this way by a colleague, someone who should have the intellectual strength and emotional resilience to know better. Abigail has not raised a formal grievance against Dr. Avery. Although she could."

He paused, allowing the impact of his words to sink in. Abigail felt a little of the tightness around her heart loosen. She didn't know if Griffin had managed to change Dr. Porter's mind. But he was on her side. He had thought about this from her perspective. He'd said he would help her fight and that was what he was doing. Win or lose, she would always remember this moment and the look in his eyes.

"I will look into this." Dr. Porter's whole body had stiffened as though concrete had been injected into his veins. "But your other objection, Dr. Matthews, that Jenna Avery is junior to you is not valid. Prior to his death, Dr. Hardin sent an email to myself and the other members of the Danvers University leadership team informing us that he was removing you from the Mem10 project with immediate effect. You were demoted and Jenna Avery was to be your replacement."

For a moment, Abigail felt as though the earth had tilted off its axis. A curious sense of acceptance came over her. So that was it. She had lost her job without even knowing. Jenna had said as much when Abigail had seen her outside Evan's office but she'd hoped it wasn't true. Jenna was incapable of doing justice to the project to which Abigail had dedicated so much of her time and expertise. And now Jenna would oversee the Anthrosyne investigation and do everything she could to implicate Abigail further.

"How long before Dr. Hardin's death did he send that email?" Griffin asked.

"I don't see why the timing is important," Dr. Porter blustered.

"It could be very important. Dr. Hardin was killed on the day he told Abigail she was being investigated. From what I've heard of him, he was a very fair, very ethical man." Dr. Porter inclined his head in agreement. "It seems odd to me that he would make the decision to replace Abigail without having even started an internal investigation into the allegations. It is even more strange that he would have informed you about it without telling her."

Dr. Porter tented his fingers beneath his chin. "What are you suggesting?"

"I think the police would like to take a look at that email, particularly in relation to the time of Dr. Hardin's death and his other activities that day."

Abigail raised a shaking hand to her throat. "Do you think it was written by someone other than Evan?"

"I'm almost certain it was," Griffin said. "And I'd like a copy of that email so I can take it to Detective Emmanuel Iglesias."

When they arrived at the Grand Rapids Police Department building, the front desk cop, Michaela Martin, recognized Griffin. Some of his cases brought him into contact with the police and, of course, his CI work meant he liaised closely with local law enforcement.

"I need to speak to Detective Iglesias," he told Michaela.

"Join the queue." She rolled her eyes and pointed to a stack of papers on the reception counter. "Those are his messages."

"It's urgent."

Something in his tone must have resonated with her because she looked from him to Abigail, then nodded. "Let me see if I can contact him." She moved away from the desk.

"Will Detective Iglesias listen to what we have to say to him?" Abigail murmured. "It all sounds so far-fetched."

"He'll listen." Griffin was now certain that who-ever killed Evan Hardin was also trying to frame Abigail. That person was determined to ruin her life and he, or she, had to be stopped. The idea of a faceless killer plotting to harm her made his blood run cold. If anything happened to her or Maya... "I'll make him."

A few minutes later, Emmanuel approached the desk. He looked tired and distracted.

"Griffin. Dr. Matthews." He nodded at them in turn. "I haven't been in touch because I don't have anything new to tell you—"

"We have some information for you," Griffin said.

"In that case, you'd better follow me."

He led them along a corridor to a small office. If the amount of paperwork on his desk was any indica-tion, Emmanuel was either very busy, or very disor-ganized. He cleared stacks of files from two chairs so that Griffin and Abigail could sit down. After mov-ing to the swivel chair behind his desk, he took out a pad and pen.

"I take it this new information relates to Dr. Har-din's murder?"

"Indirectly," Griffin said. "I told you I believed someone was trying to frame Abigail."

"That's right. You asked us to look at the son of one of her former patients." Emmanuel flipped through his notepad. "A Ryan Thorne."

Griffin drummed his fingers on the desk. "He's one of several people you need to consider. But there is new evidence of attempts to ruin Abigail's reputa-tion. If you can find out who is behind those, it might bring you closer to discovering who would make it look like she killed her boss."

Quickly, but succinctly, he outlined how he and Abigail had found out that her name had been removed from articles on the Danvers University website. "We haven't checked every report that credits Abigail. Of the few we have, we've found evidence of tampering."

"Who has administrator rights to the university website?" Emmanuel asked Abigail.

"When I've written articles for inclusion on the website, I've submitted them to Dr. Porter's personal assistant. They are then approved and uploaded to the website," she said. "I'm not sure who else has access to the website."

"I guess it could have been hacked?" Griffin suggested.

"That's something I'll need to check out." Emmanuel scribbled a note on his pad. "I agree that this appears to be a campaign against Abigail but I'm not sure it's strong enough to link it to the murder of Dr. Hardin."

"There's more." Griffin outlined the conversation they'd had less than an hour ago with Dr. Porter. "On the day of his death, Dr. Hardin allegedly sent an email to Dr. Porter and other senior colleagues. In it, he told them that he was going to demote Abigail and replace her with a junior colleague, someone who was not qualified to lead the Mem10 program."

"I can see how much this troubles you." Emmanuel

looked from Griffin to Abigail. "But I don't work in your world, so I need you to explain why."

She cleared her throat. "Evan Hardin and I had worked together for five years. He was one of the fairest men I knew, and he always upheld the high standards of the university. He had been appointed to lead an investigation into the allegation that I had used Anthrosyne in my research. He would not have taken his responsibility to me, or the university, lightly. There is no way he would have made the decision to demote and replace me before he'd even started that investigation or proven the allegations' veracity."

Emmanuel tapped his pen on his pad. "I see what you mean. If he'd done so, it would have looked like he'd already made a judgment that you were guilty."

She nodded, and Griffin could see the relief in her eyes. This police officer understood. "Exactly. And, even if he had concluded his investigation and decided that I could no longer be part of the Mem10 trial, Jenna Avery was not qualified to be my replacement. Danvers University has a small faculty, but there are half a dozen others who could have stepped in to take over my role."

She turned to look at Griffin. "I haven't told you this, but I remembered something while we were at the university. When I was in Evan's office on the day before he was murdered, he told me that, in addition to the Anthrosyne investigation, he had another equally urgent staffing matter to deal with."

"Did he give you any details?" Emmanuel asked.

"No. That was all he said."

"Have you done as I asked and checked the security camera footage of the area around Dr. Hardin's office before and after his death?" Griffin asked the detective. "We need to know if anyone entered after the first crime scene search and before the second. That would tell us who could have planted Abigail's bracelet."

"The security cameras were disabled," Emmanuel said.

"Well, isn't that convenient? Looks like someone didn't want to be seen." Griffin shifted impatiently in his seat."

"Thank you. It had occurred to me." Emmanuel turned to a clean page in his notebook. "Tell me about Dr. Avery."

"Oh, goodness. I wasn't implying—"

"I have to look at everyone involved in a case," Emmanuel said. "I'm already aware that Dr. Avery was one of the last people to talk to Dr. Hardin. Now it seems that she may have more information that can help with my inquiry."

Abigail cast a doubtful look in Griffin's direction. "No one is suggesting that you are trying to cast blame on Dr. Avery," he assured her.

The corners of her mouth turned down. "I'm not sure she would see it that way. She already hates me."

"Dr. Avery bought some RevitaYou vitamins and got sick. She blames Abigail and has been publicly confrontational with her about it," Griffin told Emmanuel.

"It certainly sounds like she has a reason to hold

a grudge against you." Emmanuel made a quick note as he spoke.

"If you're using RevitaYou as your baseline, there are a lot of people who have a reason to hold a grudge against me," Abigail said. "Does the fact that one of them happened to work with me make her more likely to be behind these attacks?"

"Maybe not. But it certainly gives her better access to the Danvers University website. And to Dr. Hardin," Emmanuel said.

"Doesn't it also mean she had a better chance of stirring things up among the families of the Mem10 participants?" Griffin asked.

Abigail frowned. "There's been no suggestion that anyone did that."

"So far," he said. "But the group who took their family members off the Mem10 program when the RevitaYou scandal broke seems to have been quite organized and vocal. I think it's worth considering whether they were being fed information from behind the scenes."

"It's something I'll look into when I speak to Ryan Thorne and the others who withdrew their family members from Mem10." Emmanuel spent a few moments reading through his notes. "I have a fairly detailed picture of Dr. Hardin's movements during his last day. Do you have a copy of the email he sent to Dr. Porter and his other colleagues? The one in which he told them he was replacing Abigail with Jenna Avery. It will be useful to place it in the time frame of what else he was doing."

Griffin took out his cell and found the email. "Dr. Porter was a little reluctant to share it with me but we told him we were coming straight here after we left his office, so he knew it would only be a matter of time before you subpoenaed his records."

He handed the phone over to Emmanuel. After reading for a minute or two, the detective looked up. "Okay. Here are my initial thoughts. We have Dr. Hardin's work laptop and his cell phone in our possession and I've already seen the messages he sent during the few days prior to his death. Although this message was sent from his Danvers University email address, it was not sent from either of those devices. Forward it to me and I'll get our technicians straight onto finding out where it *was* sent from."

"Do you agree with Griffin that there's a chance Dr. Hardin didn't send it?" Abigail asked. Without looking in Griffin's direction, she reached for his hand. When he clasped her fingers, they were cold as ice, despite the summer temperatures.

"I know he didn't send it. And the device is not my reason for saying that." Emmanuel paused, clearly weighing his words. "This is confidential, but at the time this email was sent, Dr. Hardin was undergoing emergency dental treatment. Clearly, he could not have sent the email."

"Which means that someone else did," Griffin said. "And, when you find out who it was, you'll know who is trying to frame Abigail."

Chapter 10

They drove to Heritage Hill in silence, both wrapped in their own thoughts. Abigail was relieved that Emmanuel seemed to be taking her claim that someone was trying to frame her more seriously. At the same time, it made the looming threat of a shadowy figure who wanted to harm her even more real. More than ever, she was glad of Griffin's reassuring presence.

"I don't want to launch into a full-on conspiracy theory," he said, as they approached CI headquarters. "But we have to consider the possibility that there is a group of people behind the effort to discredit you as a response to your father's criminal activity. They could have someone—not necessarily Jenna Avery— working inside the university feeding them information about you."

Abigail shivered. "That's a horrible thought."

"I'm not trying to alarm you. But the RevitaYou con has made a lot of people angry. And it's receiving attention on social media. Who knows what people are saying about your father, or how they're planning to get back at him? I'm just suggesting that we should look at all the angles." He turned his head briefly to look her way. "And we need to be prepared for them. Let's not take any chances with your safety, or Maya's."

"I could consider the possibility that people might have gotten together and plotted revenge if it wasn't for the fact that Evan has been killed," Abigail said. "That's too extreme. No matter how angry people are at what my father has done, I can't picture a situation in which a group would see that as suitable revenge."

Griffin pulled into the drive of the house where he had lived as a child and pulled up in the small parking lot at the rear. "You're right, of course. It would only take one reasonable person within the group to hear of such a plan. They would immediately report it to the police."

"So we're back to a lone person with a grudge against me?" Abigail said, as they exited the vehicle.

"I guess that was always the most likely scenario. But let's keep an open mind."

Although Riley lived in their childhood home, which also served as the CI headquarters, Griffin had already explained that the other Colton siblings still came and went as they pleased. They entered through the rear door, which led them straight into the kitchen.

"It looks remarkably tidy," Griffin said. "Maya can't have been in here."

Abigail dug him in the ribs with her elbow. "Just because *you* let a nine-month-old walk all over you…"

The sounds of laughter drew them along the hall and into the den. Riley and Charlize were both sitting on the rug with Maya. Their dog, Pal, was lying nearby, with her nose close to the baby's feet. Griffin and Abigail paused in the doorway to watch the game that was in progress. Riley passed a ball to Charlize, who then passed it to Maya. The baby took it from her but, instead of passing it to Riley, she attempted to give it to Pal.

Looking up, Charlize beckoned them into the room. "She's done this every time. It was love at first sight between Maya and Pal."

Riley grinned. "I think you might have trouble when you try to leave. Pal is convinced Maya is her puppy."

At that instant, Maya saw them. Giving a welcoming screech, she waved her hands.

"Hi, honey." Abigail scooped her up into her arms. "It looks like you've been having fun." The darkness of the day receded as her little girl snuggled close and tucked her head into Abigail's neck. When Griffin approached, Maya reached out a hand as though inviting him to share the embrace.

"Hey." As he leaned in close and stroked Maya's

cheek, Abigail could see how moved he was. "It's good to see you, too."

"She's gorgeous," Charlize said. "The sweetest little girl ever."

The two women shared a smile over Maya's head. Abigail didn't have many friends, but admiration of her baby was a surefire way to win a place among that select group. When Charlize went to make coffee, Abigail and Maya accompanied her, leaving the Colton brothers to discuss CI business.

Pal followed them and Maya, who, despite her inability to speak, was good at making her wishes known, demanded to be put down. As soon as Abigail placed her on the floor, she wiggled her way over to the dog.

"Do they all do that before they crawl?" Charlize asked.

"The wriggling like a worm? I don't think so. All babies seem to find different ways of getting around. I'm not sure if Maya will ever crawl. She gets around so fast on her belly she may stick with that until she starts walking." They watched as Maya grabbed a handful of Pal's fur in each hand and hauled herself upright. "That's one patient dog."

"Pal has to be the most good-natured canine in the world," Charlize agreed. "I only hope my baby is as good-natured as Maya." She placed a hand on her belly. "I'm blissfully happy, but this whole thing has been quite an adjustment—moving in with Riley, the pregnancy, getting engaged…"

As they watched it was as if some unspoken communication passed between the baby and the dog. Slowly, Pal took a tiny step and, still clinging to the canine's coat, Maya moved with her. Pal glanced over her shoulder as though checking the little girl was okay before repeating the action. Gradually, they made their way across the small kitchen.

"I would not have believed that if I hadn't seen it for myself," Charlize said.

"Pal sure is a special dog." Abigail shook her head. "You and Riley won't need to buy a fancy baby walker for your own little one."

They were still laughing when they returned to the den. Charlize carried a tray with the coffee cups while Abigail hoisted Maya onto her hip. Pal followed close behind, nudging Abigail on the leg every now and them as though checking that the baby was okay.

"I've been bringing Riley up to date with the latest developments in the Anthrosyne investigation and the attempts to frame you for Dr. Hardin's murder," Griffin said.

"I know these incidents don't officially form part of a CI case but, given the seriousness of the situation and the overlap with our inquiries into RevitaYou, I think we should call a team meeting." Riley's expression was somber. "Particularly since the information you have about Landon Street could prove useful to the other CI members." He turned to Abigail. "Are you happy to share all of this information with our sisters?"

"Of course." She nodded. "The circumstances

might not be ideal, but Griffin tells me that I'm part of the CI team now and that's a comforting thought."

A brief look flashed between Riley and Charlize. Although it was over in seconds, it was a lot like an I-told-you-so glance. But *what* had they been saying to each other about her? She didn't know and she certainly didn't feel comfortable asking.

"There's a lot to talk about. How about we do it over dinner tonight?" Riley asked.

"Sounds like a plan," Griffin said. He pointed to Pal, who had her head on Abigail's knee as she gazed lovingly at Maya. "And a reunion."

When they reached Griffin's apartment, he carried a sleepy Maya inside and turned to face Abigail. "I have something important to say to you."

"Goodness." She regarded him nervously. "From the look on your face it must be serious."

"It *is* a very serious subject. I think it's time."

She swallowed hard, a faint blush staining her cheeks. "For what?"

"For me to do a solo diaper change." He beckoned her closer. "And it's a stinky one."

Abigail wafted a hand under her nose. "Are you sure about this?"

"As sure as I'll ever be. You stay here while I get suited up in rubber gloves, put a clothespin on my nose, get the goggles and find a scrub top."

She giggled. "If you can laugh, you are halfway to winning the diaper battle."

"I am serious." His solemn look turned into a grin. "Just stay close by in case I need help."

She started to laugh. "From the smell, you may need reinforcements. Luckily, this little one is ready for her nap, so she may not put up a fight."

Although she was tired, Maya appeared to view those words as a challenge. Griffin carried her through to the bedroom that she shared with Abigail. As soon as he placed her on the changing table that they'd brought from Abigail's apartment, she tried to roll away from him.

Distract her, then pin her down. He remembered Abigail's tactics and handed Maya a toy. She threw it on the floor and started thrashing wildly from side to side.

"She's cranky and trying to get out of being changed," Abigail said. "Just power through and, even if she screams, remember it's for her own good."

Determinedly, Griffin got on with the task in hand. Sure enough, Maya, outraged that he refused to stop, even when she threw herself wildly around, began to cry loudly.

"This is no fun for me, you know," Griffin told her. "In fact, if we're being honest, I'm the one who should be shedding tears."

When he finally got her cleaned up and into a fresh diaper, Maya lay back on her mat and studied him with a resentful expression.

"Do you think she'll ever forgive me?" Griffin asked Abigail.

"You go and wash up while I sing her favorite

rock ballad. She'll be asleep in no time, and when she wakes up she'll have forgotten that you're the nasty man who changed her when she wanted to stay dirty."

After he'd disposed of the dirty diaper and washed his hands, he returned to the bedroom. Abigail was placing the sleeping baby in her crib. When Griffin moved to stand at her side, she placed a finger on her lips. Side by side, they watched over Maya as she slumbered.

The little girl looked so tiny with one hand tucked under her cheek and her dark curls fluffed up around her head. Griffin was blown away by the strength of the emotions that Abigail and Maya aroused in him. But it was more than that. There was a feeling of rightness to having them in his life that warmed him and scared him at the same time. Because what would happen when this was all over and they left? How would he cope with a normality that no longer contained them?

Abigail turned her head to look at him and he saw some of his own thoughts reflected in her eyes. She placed her hand over his where it rested on the wooden rail of the crib.

"I'm not good at this." Why did he always have to spoil things by explaining?

"At what?" Her voice was husky.

"Everything." He resisted the temptation to groan. "Life. Relationships…"

"Is that what this is?" She moved a fraction closer. "A relationship? I wouldn't know, you see. I've never been in one."

"Nor have I. Not really. I don't know how to relate to other people on a personal level—"

She placed a finger on his lips. "Can we stop talking now?"

"I think we should."

He caught hold of her around the waist, moving her backward away from the crib.

"Wait." Abigail stopped him before they reached the door.

He released her immediately. "Is this not okay?"

"It's more than okay." She smiled up at him. "It's wonderful. But spontaneity and babies don't mix."

"Ah." He returned the smile. "Bring the baby monitor to my room."

She rose on the tips of her toes to kiss him. "Any man who can say that at a time like this definitely knows how to relate to people on a personal level."

The few minutes between Griffin entering his bedroom and Abigail following him in felt like a lifetime. They also gave him just enough time for the doubts to set in. He closed the drapes and started pacing. This had to be a bad idea. Even if they discounted everything that was happening, neither of them was relationship material.

Who said this is leading to a relationship?

He couldn't argue his way out of things that easily. This wasn't about sex. He almost laughed out loud at the thought. *Not about sex? So why are we sneaking into my room in the middle of the day while the baby is asleep?* That wasn't the point. The physical attraction between them was undeniable but there was so much more to it.

Even if they weren't falling for each other deeper and deeper with each passing day, they were living under the same roof and sharing the care of Maya. They couldn't rush into anything...

"I'm sorry," Abigail whispered, as she closed the door behind her. "Maya stirred and I thought she was waking up."

Then she was walking toward him and every thought went out of his head except the need to take her into his arms. Heat flared between them as soon as they kissed. When they broke apart, Abigail reached for his hand, leading him toward the bed.

"Wait." She stopped, her expression questioning. "Are you sure about this?"

"Totally." Her gaze scanned his face. "Are you?"

"Yes." And he was. The doubts of a few minutes ago were gone. "I've never been more certain of anything in my life."

Her smile was radiant. "What a lovely thing to say."

As he looked down at her, it hit him. There was no need to be afraid. This beautiful woman wanted him as much as he wanted her. And right here, right now, that was all that mattered. The future could wait.

With a soft growl, he lifted her off her feet and carried her to the bed. Before he could place her on it, Abigail put a hand on his chest.

"I want to see you." Even though the light was dim, he could see the color that stained her cheeks. "All of you."

"Works both ways."

Shyness and patience were forgotten as, within minutes, they removed their clothes and lay facing each other on the bed. Abigail wrapped her arms around Griffin's neck, pressing the length of her body tight to his.

"This feels very, very good."

Pushing her arms above her head, he gently eased her onto her back and knelt between her legs. Pausing for a second, he checked her face, looking for any signs of hesitation. Her figured that her half-closed eyes and the way she slowly ran her tongue over her bottom lip were encouraging.

Then she whispered, "I want you." It was the only signal he needed.

Dropping his forehead onto hers, he pressed a lingering kiss onto her lips. Abigail wrapped her long legs around his hips and pulled her body up to meet his, rubbing against him. Griffin gripped her thighs, caressing them before moving his fingers closer to her core.

A little moan escaped Abigail's lips as she fisted the sheets on either side of her hips. "Oh, please…" Her voice was a hoarse rasp.

"Please what?"

"Please touch me."

"I am touching you." He smiled into her eyes.

"Ah, Griffin. Don't tease me." She looked down the length of her body at him. "Please touch me *there*."

"You mean here?"

Leaning forward, he took one long lick at her center. Abigail cried out, her head falling back on the pillow as her whole body trembled. Holding her steady with his hands on her hips, Griffin swiped his tongue through her folds, over and over. Burying her hands in his hair, she thrashed wildly, grinding her hips up toward his face.

"Oh, oh." Her cries echoed around the room.

Grasping her thighs tightly, he parted her legs wider before taking her clit in his mouth. As he sucked, then flicked his tongue across the surface of the sensitive flesh, Abigail came apart.

"Griffin!"

She was jerking and shaking as he held her down, murmuring in pleasure at her reaction. After a minute or two, she reached up and wrapped her arms around his neck, pulling him down into a kiss. He groaned into her mouth, tilting their heads so that he could kiss her deeper and harder, his own desire burning further out of control.

"I almost forgot." Abigail raised her head to look at him. "Do you have protection?"

"Yes." He leaned across and reached into the top drawer of his nightstand.

She trailed a hand down his body. "Then I think we should use it."

Abigail couldn't believe that the amazing orgasm Griffin had just given her with his mouth had only partly satisfied her. Only minutes later, she wanted to feel him driving into her, their bodies slick with perspiration, their hearts pounding in time. This wild side to her personality was as new as it was unexpected. But she knew she could trust Griffin and maybe that was why she was able to let go of her inhibitions with him.

Moving her hands down Griffin's body, she gripped his taut ass and pulled him tight against her. The moment their hips met, and she shifted beneath him, a groan rumbled deep in his chest. The depth of emotion in his eyes took her breath away.

"I didn't know it was possible to feel this alive." As he tore open the condom packet, she sensed he was having trouble speaking.

Abigail moved one hand down between their bodies and stroked his hard, throbbing shaft. "So big."

He thrust his hips, moving in her grip. "Any more of that kind of talk and I'll be so turned on the condom will be a waste of time."

"Then maybe I should help you with that?"

She rubbed her thumb across his head before taking the latex sheath from him. Using one hand to pinch the top of the condom at the tip with her thumb and forefinger, she rolled the condom down while stroking his length. From the way Griffin drew in a sharp breath, she figured he approved of her technique.

He leaned toward her and kissed her mouth, and she wrapped her legs around his back, opening herself up to him. She could taste herself on his lips, but she could also taste *him*. And she loved his flavor.

He moved his right hand down, guiding himself

to her and she tilted her pelvis. As he slowly pushed into her, then retreated again, she gasped at the sensation of him filling her. It was so intense and pleasurable that her inner muscles spasmed just at that first entry. She gripped his waist, holding on tight as he drove deeper each time.

Her body was on fire, the flames starting at the point where their bodies connected and blazing a path along her nerve endings. Whimpering in frustration, she ground her lower body tighter against his. Lifting his head, he smiled into her eyes before pulling back slightly. Holding him tighter, she jerked upward, trying to force him to go harder and faster.

In response to her action, he kissed her deep. As she sucked on his tongue, he lost some of his control. His hips bucked and he plunged wildly in and out.

"Yes." Throwing her head back, Abigail arched her back.

He surged forward, filling her completely before holding still. She loved the feeling of every inch of him pressed into her sensitive inner walls. But the longer he held himself still deep, the more she needed the motion of him powering into her, rubbing his flesh against hers.

She lifted her hips, pleasuring his length with her body and chasing her own fulfillment at the same time. She was so close. Maddeningly, deliciously close. Griffin moved in time with her upward motion, and her body started to convulse. She cried out, holding on tight to Griffin's forearms. As he let go of all restraints, her body spasmed around him and she welcomed every thrust.

She tightened her inner muscles around him as light and color exploded through her body. After a moment, Griffin jerked and cried out as his own climax hit.

Wanting to keep the connection between them for as long as possible, she wrapped her arms around his waist. He bowed his head into the curve of her neck and they remained still, breathing hard for several minutes. When he finally collapsed on the bed beside her, Abigail turned toward him, tucking her body tight against his. She could hear the pounding of his heart against her ear as he stroked her hair.

She felt curiously conflicted. Her body was at peace, but she wanted to laugh and cry at the same time. It was as if a cork had been popped and her emotions had come pouring out like champagne from a bottle.

Griffin was her rock in a stormy sea. He was the only person she trusted. Now he had become so much more than that. What had happened between them was so much more than sex. She hid a smile against his chest. *Although the sex was pretty amazing.* It had confirmed everything she'd hoped and feared.

She wasn't falling for Griffin Colton. She'd already fallen.

Chapter 11

"I think I should try looking after Maya on my own.,
Griffin said the next morning. He looked like a man
who couldn't quite believe he'd said those words out
loud.

Abigail gave him a doubtful glance. "What am
I supposed to do while you two have a little bonding time?"

"Anything you want to. Take a bath. Read a maga-
zine. Go for a walk."

"A bath would be nice," she said longingly. "I can't
remember the last time I soaked in some scented bubbles."

"That's settled." He placed a hand at the small of her
back and steered her toward the door. "We'll be fine."

Before she left the room, she looked back over her

shoulder. Griffin was seated on the rug with Maya and the baby was trying to poke him in the eye. Of course, they'd be fine.

Griffin's master bathroom had a huge roll-top tub and Abigail eyed it with pleasure as she turned on the faucet. She'd just removed her clothes and was preparing to step into the steaming water when Griffin yelled for her.

"Abigail! Come quickly."

The panic in his voice had her running naked into the den.

"There's something wrong with Maya." He was on his feet, his face ashen as he pointed to the baby. "I think she's having a seizure."

Maya was lying on her back on the rug. Every few seconds, her body would jerk and her spine would arch upward from the floor. Each time it happened, she let out a squeak. When Abigail knelt beside her, the little girl grinned at her, then rolled away. The jerking and squeaking continued as she moved.

Abigail bit back a smile, determined to reassure Griffin instead of laughing at him. "There is nothing wrong with Maya. She has the hiccups."

"Seriously?" He ran a hand through his hair. "That's all it is?"

She nodded. "It happens a lot."

He started to laugh. "I guess I overreacted a little."

Abigail got to her feet. "Just a little." She raised an eyebrow as his gaze roamed over her body. "What are you doing?"

His eyes twinkled. "Just admiring the view."

She wagged a finger at him. "That's not allowed when you're minding the baby."

He held up his hands. "I was only looking."

"How about you look in that direction?" She pointed at Maya, who was on her way out of the door. "And let me get back to my bath?"

Muttering an apology, he hurried to retrieve the baby while Abigail returned to the bathroom. While she knew that Maya would be fine with Griffin, she spent most of her "me time" listening for the sounds of chaos.

Although there were a few bumps and thuds, she didn't hear anything that caused her any alarm. Finally, she relaxed and lay back in the scented bubbles. Half an hour later, she emerged. After taking time to dry her hair and dress in clean sweatpants and a T-shirt, she wandered downstairs.

"That was wonder—" she broke off. "What happened here?"

Griffin's den looked like a scene from a disaster movie. An earthquake, or possibly a hurricane, Abigail decided as she surveyed the scene. Possibly even the aftermath of a nuclear explosion.

Griffin was seated on the floor, picking up the pieces of a shattered picture frame. He looked like a man who had stared into the abyss and no longer had anything left to fear. For some reason, his hair was wet. Maya was trapped in a corner between the coffee table and a chair, but she seemed happy enough as she bashed one of her dolls over the head with a rattle.

"Her diaper was dirty," Griffin said. "I mean, industrial-level dirty. So I started to change her. I was doing a good job until I realized I didn't have a bag to put the dirty one in." He closed his eyes briefly. "I only moved away for a second. Just long enough to get a bag."

Abigail placed a hand on his shoulder. "Don't tell me. She got the dirty diaper?"

"You've been there?"

"I think most parents have." Her voice was sympathetic.

"There was poop everywhere." He shuddered at the memory. "All over Maya, the rug, the sofa, the TV. And, when I tried to stop her, she grabbed me by the hair."

"Oh, Griffin."

"Abigail…" His eyes were round with horror. "I had baby poop in my *hair*."

She sat on the floor next to him, picking up a few shards of glass that he'd missed. "What did you do?"

"You mean when I'd stopped retching?" She nodded. "I took her through to my room and we both got into the shower. Then I cleaned up in here. I tried to hold onto Maya with one hand but she still grabbed a few things and tried to trash the place."

"So, um, did you enjoy looking after her on your own?"

He gave her a suspicious look. "Are you laughing at me?"

She tried to keep a straight face, but the laughter bubbled up. "Maybe a little."

Griffin stared at her in disbelief for a moment or

two, then a slight smile touched his lips. "It would have been just my luck if John Jones had arrived while this place was Poop City."

"At least if the police had turned up to arrest me, the stink might have put them off." Abigail leaned against him, chuckling.

As they toppled onto the rug, giggling uncontrollably, Maya, who was clearly tired of being left out, threw her rattle at them.

Although Charlize had made a chicken casserole, Griffin noticed each of his siblings brought a contribution to the evening meal. As a result, the table was overloaded with food at the family dinner that took place before the CI meeting. Maya, who was refreshed after a long nap, ate even more than usual and enjoyed having an audience.

Maya was seated on Griffin's knee and he stopped her as she leaned over and offered the dog a piece of cornbread. "No, don't give that to Pal." Giving him a radiant smile, she carefully rubbed her buttery fingers over the front of his shirt instead. "Thank you for sharing."

He looked up to find his sisters watching them. All four of them wore the same expression. It reminded him of the way they'd looked when they were kids and the family cat had given birth to a litter of kittens.

"You're so sweet," Sadie said.

Griffin got the feeling she was talking to him as well as Maya. Ordinarily, he'd have been uncomfortable at being the center of attention but, all of a sudden, he got it. This was what it was all about. This was family. His sisters were watching him interact with his little girl.

His little girl? Where had that come from? He was fostering Maya on a temporary basis to help Abigail through a difficult period in her life. There had never been any suggestion that it would become anything more. He knew, from his foster parent training, that it would be easy to form bonds with a child in his care. He also knew that, when the time came, he would have to let go. But this felt different.

He knew why. It was because of Abigail. He looked across the table at where she was talking to Charlize and his heart constricted. He'd never known emotion like this existed. And it terrified him. Because he didn't know how to deal with it. All his life, he'd maintained a distance from those around him, scared that his craving for love would be overpowering.

He'd told himself that dating was enough. He didn't want more than a casual relationship now and then. But in Abigail, he'd met a woman who had turned his whole life upside down. A woman who'd made him rethink everything he knew about himself. Because now he knew exactly what he wanted. He wanted her. And Maya. He wanted a family. He wanted *everything*. And with that knowledge, the old doubts resurfaced. Was this about her? Or his longing for love? How would he ever know the difference?

When he held her in his arms, when he kissed her, and drove deep inside her, his fears vanished. In those instants, she was his and there was no need for words. It was when he tried to rationalize his feelings. That was when he was transported back to the night his mom died and he just knew that everyone would be snatched away from him sooner or later. So why bother with love? It was so much easier to do without it.

"Ugh." He was brought back to reality as Maya seized a handful of his hair and tugged hard.

"Hey." Moving swiftly around the table, Abigail came to his rescue. "That is no way to treat Griffin after everything he's done for us. His hair has been traumatized enough for one day."

She leaned against his shoulder as she released him from Maya's eye-wateringly tight grip. Her hair tickled his cheek and her scent invaded his nostrils. As she turned her head to smile at him, he knew his own warnings were a waste of time. He was lost in her, sinking deeper by the minute, and enjoying every second.

After dinner had been cleared away, the family gathered around the table once more for a business meeting. Abigail had brought toys for Maya, and the baby played happily on the rug with her wooden animals.

Griffin started the CI meeting with a summary of what had happened since the team last got together. There were shocked faces around the table as he gave his sisters more details about the murder of Evan Hardin and the various attempts to frame, or discredit Abigail.

"Surely the police can't seriously believe that Abigail killed her boss?" Pippa asked.

Griffin shrugged. "You know what a police inquiry is like. It takes time for them to examine every lead."

"An anonymous note and a bracelet found in Dr. Hardin's office?" Kiely shook her head. "It's not enough evidence for them to consider Abigail as a suspect."

"The police haven't gone that far," Griffin said. "To be fair to Detective Iglesias, he is pursuing every angle."

"Good. Because I'll be asking him to track down a certain research scientist." As he spoke, Riley held up his electronic tablet to show his siblings a photograph. "I've had no luck finding him so far."

The image was of a tall man with a beer belly. His blond-gray hair was tousled, and his blue eyes peered at the camera from behind silver wire-rimmed glasses.

"This is Dr. Landon Street. He is credited by Wes Matthews in his glossy brochure as the person who devised the RevitaYou formula."

Vikki pulled a doubtful face. "I know it's only one picture, but he does not look like someone I'd trust to design a brand-new vitamin that people would take hoping it will change their lives."

"Your instinct would be right," Riley said. "Abigail has first-hand knowledge of Landon Street's dubious methods, but the guy has basically broken every rule there is. It's a miracle that he's avoided jail. He appears to have been saved each time by his employers' reluctance to draw attention to their own shoddy practices. Rather than face justice, he quietly moved on and, as a result, he's continued his dodgy behavior in the next place. Then the next. In the case of Revita-You, his carelessness has reached the point where someone might die as a result."

"Is this because of the ricin you found in the pills?" Sadie asked Abigail.

"Yes. Ricin is an extremely deadly, naturally oc-curring poison found in castor beans. It can be cre-ated from by-products of the making of castor oil. The compound Landon Street created and added to RevitaYou causes cell death and does wonders for smoothing wrinkles. Not everyone who ingests it will die and they will look younger."

"But they're dicing with death," Sadie said.

"Exactly." Abigail nodded. "We don't know who, and we don't know when, but people will die as a re-sult of the ricin compound in RevitaYou."

"Do we know how Wes Matthews and Landon Street met?" Vikki asked. "Have they been friends for a long time, or did they only make contact recently?"

"As far as I know, they didn't know each other when Landon worked at Danvers University," Abigail said. "Neither of them mentioned knowing the other to me and I think Landon probably would have. He'd find any excuse to chat rather than work."

"Landon offered his services as a freelance re-searcher." Riley found a web page and again held it up so that everyone could see it. "Is that something you've seen before, Abigail?"

"I'm not familiar with it, but I guess there are independents in every profession. It's a worrying thought, however, because there would be no one to regulate the services offered on a site like that."

"Clearly." Riley nodded. "I compared Landon to some comparable experts. His credentials didn't match up but he was cheap. I'm guessing that would be the appeal for Wes."

"So we figure Wes went shopping for a scientist to make him some vitamins. He came across that site and he found Landon. They agreed on a price and Landon made him the formula for RevitaYou." Griffin shook his head. "It was that easy for them to come up with a product that could kill people?"

"Yes. We know the FDA hasn't seen RevitaYou, so Wes's customers didn't have that protection," Pippa said. "Although it would never have reached the marketplace, of course."

"I don't think Wes and Landon set out to kill anyone." Vikki sent a sympathetic glance in Abigail's direction.

"But they didn't care if they did," she replied. "Don't worry. I know what my father is."

"And now Landon is missing. Just like Wes," Kiely said. "Could they be together?"

"Since we don't know where Wes is either, it wouldn't help us if they were." Riley ran a hand through his hair in frustration.

"I've been trying to think of places my dad might go." Abigail withdrew a folded piece of paper from the pocket of her jeans. "He was born in Michigan and spent most of his life here, but I think he would move on if he felt cornered here. My mom was from Cuba, but they met here in Grand Rapids. They were divorced and I don't think he had anything to do with her family after she died, but I suppose it's always possible that he could have made contact with them." She moved her finger down the list she'd written. "He used to talk about his cousins who lived in Texas, but I don't know where exactly. I know that's not helpful."

"It's very helpful." Griffin covered her hand with his. "It gives us a starting point."

"There was something else. It may be nothing, but he always talked about wanting to go deep sea fishing." She looked around the table. Each of the Colton siblings was watching her with understanding and support. For the first time since her mom had walked out, she felt included. Even wanted. "I just wondered if he might go to a place where he could hide away on a boat. I'm sorry. I know it's a big world out there, with a lot of boats…"

"Any information you can give us is helpful," Riley told her. "We can start looking at whether Wes made travel arrangements in the past, or if he knew anyone who organized boat charters."

"We also have to consider that Wes might do the exact opposite of what is expected and choose a place no one would ever think to look for him," Griffin said.

"On that subject, FBI agent Cooper Winston, who is working the RevitaYou case, has asked me to call him. I'll do that now so that you can all hear the conversation."

The others waited in silence while Riley contacted

the Grand Rapids field office. When he got through to Agent Winston, the two men exchanged greetings.

"Cooper, I'm in a CI meeting with my siblings. Wes Matthews's daughter, Abigail, is also here and so is my fiancée, Charlize Kent. Is it okay if I put you on speaker phone?"

Once he'd secured the other man's agreement, Riley continued the call so that everyone in the room could hear. "We've been discussing likely places Matthews might hide."

"Since there's no sign of him, we have to assume that he's living under an alias and in disguise," Cooper said.

"If that's the case, we need to come up with a way to trap him or lure him back to Grand Rapids." Griffin's patience appeared to be wearing thin. It was clear he wanted a resolution and was frustrated that they couldn't find one. Abigail was touched to realize that it was for her sake.

"We'll keep trying to find him." From the weary note in Cooper's voice, the FBI were experiencing the same level of annoyance. "I'll let you know as soon as I have any information for you."

"We'll do the same," Riley said. Before he ended the call, he let Cooper know what they'd learned about Landon Street and promised to follow the details up in an email.

After Riley ended the call, the mood was despondent. It seemed that the RevitaYou investigation was stalling. No one had heard from Brody, and the siblings were growing increasingly worried about his well-being.

"We should consider two possibilities in regard to contact between Wes and Landon Street," Griffin said. "Either they are still in touch and watching out for each other, or the stress of the investigation and the social media campaign has driven them apart. Either way, if one of them is caught, we should use that against the other."

"What do you mean?" Sadie asked.

"If Landon is arrested first, we should put out a social media blast saying that he's given police details about Wes, even if it's not true. And vice versa."

"Good thinking." Kiely nodded. "Play the bad guys off against each other."

"We have to catch one of them first, remember?" Pippa covered her mouth as she yawned. "Sorry, guys. I had an early start this morning."

It was the cue for the meeting to wind down and, after exchanging a few more details, the siblings started to leave. Abigail gathered up Maya's toys and carried the baby through to the kitchen to thank Charlize. After a few minutes, Griffin joined them.

"Are you ready to go home?"

She had never heard a sweeter question. For a moment her throat constricted. Then she managed a smile. "Home sounds like the best idea ever."

When Maya was asleep, Abigail joined Griffin in his bed. Wrapping her arms around his neck, she twisted her fingers in the hair that grew slightly longer over his nape to draw him closer. His tongue licked hungrily over the seam of her lips, and her mouth parted eagerly for him. He slanted his lips over hers, holding the back of her head and tilting her into a kiss that became hard and deep.

Need surged through her, wild and wanton. She had never felt like this before, and she welcomed it, her need for him escalating, spiraling out of control until she was shaking with the intensity of it.

Griffin jerked his head back and stared at her, his eyes gleaming with a hunger that scared and delighted her.

"I want you more than I have ever wanted anything in my life." His voice was hoarse with need.

She drew his head back down to hers, brushing her lips against his, triggering a series of hungry kisses. She couldn't get enough of him. Couldn't get close enough to him. She needed his tongue in her mouth, the hard muscles of his chest against the softness of her too-sensitive breasts, his hands exploring her body. She needed everything he could give her. Measured and gentle wouldn't do. Self-control wasn't good enough. What Abigail wanted there and then was raw and out of control.

Griffin eased her down so that they were lying side by side and she pressed her hips tight to his until the heavy ridge of his erection pressed firmly against the intimate mound between her thighs. Her hands slid to his chest, her fingers trembling as they slid through the crisp hair. Hunger raged out of control throughout her body. She was intoxicated by the sensual storm gripping her.

Griffin tugged her T-shirt up, and she raised her arms so he could pull it over her head and cast it aside. Her bra followed and his lips were an impatient heat against her nipples as he drew first one delicate tip, then the other, into his mouth. Abigail arched her back and cried out, as a whole new spectrum of sensation swept over her. She was spinning out of control, giving herself up to rapture.

She ran her hand down the front of his body, smoothing over the hard muscles of his chest and down over the ridges of his abdomen. Griffin sucked in a breath as her fingertips lightly brushed his straining erection.

Giving a shaky laugh, he took hold of her hand and guided it so she could wrap her fingers around his shaft. He was raw, pulsing heat beneath her touch. "That feels like heaven but it may test my self-control to the limit."

As she caressed his warm flesh, Griffin's hand moved inside the elastic of her sweat pants, one finger parting her swollen folds. Abigail gave a gasp and he paused. "Is that okay?"

She nodded vigorously. "It's wonderful."

"Then let's get rid of these." She raised her hips so that he could pull her sweatpants and underwear down over her hips and legs.

She let her eyes wander down his body. He was so big and hard, his erection heavy and straining toward her. His silken flesh looked like it was made to be stroked. She knelt on the bed, moving toward him on her knees.

"Let me taste you."

She wrapped her fingers around the base of his shaft and lowered her head, swiping her tongue over the engorged tip. Griffin's whole body jerked, and he hissed in a breath. Abigail gave a little hum of pleasure.

"You like that?"

His groan told her that he did. Repeating the action, she flicked her tongue back and forth over the throbbing crest. His flesh tasted clean and salty, yet darkly erotic. As she became more adventurous and closed her mouth over his head, Griffin moaned, thrusting in small movements against her lips. It seemed natural to suck, and he fisted a hand in her hair in response. Abigail looked up at his face, enjoying his response. His eyes were half-closed, the cords of muscle in his neck standing out.

Gently he eased away from her. "I don't want this to be over before we've even started."

Placing his knee on the bed, he tipped her onto her back. Pressing her onto the bed, he lowered his head between her thighs, and her senses went wild. His tongue rasped over her most tender flesh with the lightest, softest strokes, licking at her, and she writhed in ecstasy, burning to lift herself closer.

"Please…" She needed more but her voice didn't seem to be working.

Luckily, Griffin seemed to know what her wail of need meant. His tongue found the tiny bundle of sensitized nerve endings and flickered over it, sending fire pulsing through her. She dug her hands into his hair in an attempt to draw him even closer. His hands hooked under her knees, pushing them back and wider apart as his tongue stroked her entrance. She felt a pressure, then he was probing just inside her. Color flamed in her cheeks. It was so sweetly, deliciously exciting.

An aching need was building inside her, hunger driving her toward a longed-for release. His lips covered her, his tongue returning to torment that tiny nub, and Abigail's whole body exploded. It propelled her into a cataclysmic ecstasy, tightening her muscles and sending shooting stars of rapture through to every cell in her body. Griffin held her down as she writhed and convulsed, calling out his name deliriously.

She became vaguely aware of him tearing open a condom wrapper before moving in place between her thighs. His lips were gentle on hers as she felt the heavy pressure of him pushing against her still-throbbing entrance.

"Don't go slow." She lifted her hips to accommodate him, gasping as her muscles began to stretch, easing the way for his steel-hard erection. "I want you…all of you."

A powerful thrust of his hips pushed him deeper into her, the tight friction causing her to arch up to him. She twisted mindlessly beneath him, demanding more, and Griffin pulled back before driving into her again, seating himself fully inside her this time. She was as full as she could be. Full of him. It was glorious. Now she needed him to move. To pound in and out of her. Until she screamed.

She wrapped her legs around his hips, urging him on, and heard his groan of surrender. He drew back, then filled her again, impaling her on his thick length. Mindless pleasure washed over her. She gave herself up to sensation. Reality was lost as Griffin drove into her hard and fast, exactly as she had begged.

His erection was a hot length of iron powering into her, rubbing over tender tissue, building the friction, stoking the pleasure, until Abigail thought she might go wild. Her breath was suspended, meaning she couldn't even scream as he increased the tempo, his rapid-fire thrusts driving her ever closer to the edge.

This time, when her release slammed into her, her muscles gripped him, heightening the intensity of each spasm. It felt like liquid velvet had been poured into her veins. Her body was languid, yet every sense was heightened as she pulsed and contracted, each perfect wave ebbing and flowing rapturously over and around her.

She felt his hard flesh stiffen further, his body jerking to a standstill as the white-hot force of his own release claimed him. Abigail wrapped her arms around him, wanting to hold him to her, to capture the moment for all eternity.

Eventually she collapsed beneath him, shuddering in the aftershocks of unimaginable pleasure.

"That was…" When her breath returned, she floundered, searching for the right words.

"Perfect." He sighed the word against her ear as he drew her into his arms.

"It was."

"I meant you. *You* are perfect."

The next morning, Griffin woke early. His arms were full of Abigail's warm curves and, for a few minutes, he just enjoyed how that felt. Waking up with her was too new, too perfect, to rush. Then he remembered what he'd been thinking about the previous night and he eased carefully away from her.

Going into the kitchen, he made himself a cup of coffee before heading for his study. Once he was logged in to his laptop, he accessed the Danvers University website. He figured he could have asked Abigail for the information he was looking for but for some reason he wanted to do the research himself.

The lab's staff members were all listed under their individual faculties. Although Dr. Hardin's profile remained in place, there was a banner above the research department with an obituary honoring him and the work he had done at the university. Griffin scrolled down, studying the photographs and biographies. He wasn't sure what he was looking for. There was just something at the back of his mind that told him that they were overcomplicating things. The reason for Evan Hardin's death would turn out to be much simpler than they realized.

He skimmed past Abigail's biography, moving on to the junior staff in the department. One of the names caught his eye. Dr. Jenna Avery. What was her role in this? Why had Evan Hardin, or someone acting on his behalf, tried to use this woman to get at Abigail? Her profile was respectable, and he glanced at her photograph. Then he looked again. She was early thirties, pretty, with her dark hair cut in a short bob. And she looked familiar. But surely it couldn't be...

Quickly, he opened another tab and scrolled through his emails, finding the one that he'd sent to Liam Desmond about the online adoption scam. There it was. The old profile picture that Griffin had taken from Dr. Anne Jay's old social media account. The head of MorningStar Families was half-turned away from the camera, and the angle wasn't good, but Griffin was almost certain that Anne Jay and Jenna Avery were the same person.

"Damn it." He ran a hand through his hair. "Even the name is a clue."

Yet... Surely no one would be that arrogant? If Jenna Avery was the person behind this scam, would she really use an alias whose initials were the reverse of her own first name? It seemed too obvious, yet his job and his involvement in CI had taught him that there were no surprises when it came to criminal behavior. People who thought they were above the law often believed they were so clever that they could afford to make jokes at the expense of their victims and the law enforcement agencies who pursued them.

Even so, he was having trouble picturing anyone leading such a bizarre double life. Respectable research scientist and online fraudster? The two didn't fit well together. It was like picturing a librarian who was also a bank robber, or an accountant who mugged old ladies. Stranger things might happen, but it was hard to imagine what they might be.

An internet search didn't give him much more information about Jenna Avery than her Danvers University profile. He glanced at the time on his laptop screen. It was still early. He could wake Abigail, but did he really want to take these suspicions to her and alarm her before he'd even fully thought them through? There was one person who could always be counted on to listen without judging.

"Riley? I need to run the wildest idea by you." It was only when he heard the murmur of voices that Griffin remembered that his brother now lived with Charlize. "Sorry. Did I wake you?"

"Yeah. But it's okay." Riley yawned. "Tell me what this is about."

Quickly, Griffin outlined his thinking about Jenna Avery. "I'm being overimaginative, right? It couldn't possibly be the same woman."

"Send me the picture and the link to the university website. I'll take a look and call you back."

While he waited for his brother to check out the information he'd sent, Griffin reread the email he'd sent to Liam Desmond. As part of his investigation, Griffin had researched MorningStar Families. Despite glowing references on social media, he had been unable to find evidence that the company actually existed, or that it had helped any families to adopt. He had concluded that it existed only as a means of conning people like Liam and Shelby, who were desperate to have a child of their own.

Riley called back five minutes later. "I agree that both pictures could be the same woman, but it's not conclusive. The best thing to do is hand them over to Detective Iglesias. The police have specialist imaging equipment with which they can make a comparison."

Griffin rubbed a hand over his face. "It feels like this whole case is based on hunches and suppositions. Whenever I talk to the police, I sense them rolling their eyes."

"If you're right about this, they'll be glad you persisted," Riley said. "In the meantime, maybe you and I should have a chat with Dr. Jenna Avery."

Chapter 12

It was lunchtime and the Danvers University campus was busy as Griffin drove around the parking lot a few times before he finally found a space.

"There are no guarantees that Jenna Avery will see us," he said, as he and Riley exited the car.

"No, but Jenna said that the RevitaYou vitamins she bought made her sick," Riley reminded him. "We'll tell her that we are interviewing all victims of the con, whether they are investors, or those who have been unwell as a result of taking the pills. She felt strongly enough about it to confront Abigail publicly, so hopefully she will be willing to talk to us about her experience."

Once inside the building, they approached the desk and asked for Dr. Avery. The receptionist took their names and Riley's business card, then spoke on the telephone.

"Dr. Avery is on her way," she told them, when she ended her call.

Even without her name badge, the woman who stepped out of the elevator a few minutes later was instantly recognizable from her profile on the university website. Jenna Avery was petite and attractive, but Griffin sensed she had a watchful air about her. The receptionist handed her Riley's business card and pointed to where the Colton brothers were standing.

Jenna dug her hands into the pockets of her white lab coat as she approached. "I can only spare a few minutes, so it would be helpful if you could tell me straight away what this is about."

"My brother and I are working with the police and the FBI to bring those behind the RevitaYou con to justice," Riley said.

Her expression was hard to read but Griffin saw something shift in the dark depths of her eyes, as though she was weighing up how she could make the most of this situation.

"I can take my lunch early, if you don't mind joining me while I grab a coffee and a sandwich."

There were a few places to eat around the campus and Jenna led them to a small coffee shop. Although the place was busy, they got a table in a quiet corner. Once they'd placed their order, Jenna gave the two men a thoughtful look. "Why have you come to me to talk about RevitaYou?"

"We are talking to everyone who has had a bad experience with the vitamins," Griffin said.

"But how did you know I'd had a problem with the product? I haven't been to the police. I haven't even tried to make a complaint to the manufacturers." There it was again. That manner of hers was more than watchful. It was suspicious.

Griffin thought for a moment about the best way to answer her question. They already knew she was antagonistic toward Abigail. If he introduced her into the conversation too early, he risked driving Jenna away. "We spoke to someone else at the university who'd had a bad experience with RevitaYou. They mentioned that you'd spoken publicly about your own issues."

"Issues." Her eyes narrowed slightly. "Is that what they called it? Yes, I had issues with RevitaYou."

"Could you tell us what happened?" Riley asked.

"I bought some of the pills, took them and got sick." She shrugged. "Isn't that what happens to most people?"

"Actually, no," Griffin said. "Many RevitaYou users report no side effects."

Their server arrived with Jenna's lunch and their drinks and they waited until he had left before resuming the conversation.

"How soon after you started taking the pills did your symptoms start?" Griffin asked.

"Look." Jenna sat up straighter. "The only reason I agreed to talk to you is because I want that con man,

Wes Matthews, and his high-and-mighty daughter to get what's coming to them."

To get what's coming to them. Was it a coincidence that they were the words that Ryan Thorne had used when he threatened Abigail? There was something about Jenna that felt off to Griffin. It was as if everything about her was fake.

"The police have no reason to believe that Abigail Matthews is involved in the RevitaYou fraud." Griffin kept his voice deliberately calm. "Do you have any evidence to suggest otherwise?"

Color flared in her cheeks. "Only what I know of her. That she pretends to be better than the rest of us, yet she wouldn't miss an opportunity to betray a friend—" she broke off. "I think this conversation is over."

Griffin got to his feet. An idea had occurred to him and he just hoped Riley would see what he was doing and go along with it. "Just one more thing."

Jenna gave him a resentful glance. "What is it?"

"What did you do with your unused RevitaYou pills?"

"I threw them in the trash. Why?"

"Oh, no reason. I just hoped we could take them from you for analysis." He half turned away and then looked back. "I suppose the pretty RevitaYou bottles were just too attractive to resist."

Jenna paused in the act of taking a sip of coffee. "What do you mean?"

"I was simply surprised that a scientist would purchase an unlicensed product like RevitaYou. But then the packaging and marketing were very appealing." He smiled. "Especially the pink bottles."

Out of the corner of his eye, he saw Riley frown. His brother knew, of course, that the RevitaYou bottles were green, not pink. He gave Riley a pleading look. *Stick with me on this.*

Jenna shrugged. "We've all fallen for a product that looks good now and then."

"I guess we have. Thank you for your time, Dr. Avery."

They left the building and made their way outside. It was only when they reached the parking lot that Riley placed a hand on Griffin's shoulder.

"Nice work. She has never seen a RevitaYou pill bottle, has she?"

"No." Griffin's lips hardened into a line. "So why does she have a grudge against Abigail?"

Abigail listened in silence as Griffin recounted the details of his and Riley's meeting with Jenna Avery. As he was speaking, tiny darts of panic prickled her skin. How had her life gone so wildly off course in such a short space of time? Luckily, Maya was napping, and they had a half hour or more of quiet in which they could talk without interruption.

"I don't understand. Are you saying that she didn't know what color the RevitaYou bottles are?" she asked at last. "If she used them, she must have known that they're green."

"Exactly. Your dad did a good job of marketing his product. Those bottles are very distinctive. If Jenna had bought any RevitaYou vitamins, there is no way she would get confused about the color of the bottle." Griffin took her hand. "For some reason, she made up the whole story about getting sick as a result of taking the pills."

Abigail shook her head. "Why would she do that?"

"I can only think of one reason. Jenna must be the person who wants to get at you."

"But why?" Abigail's head was spinning. "We were friends. I wasn't close with her like I was with Veronica, but we got on. I never had any reason to suspect that she disliked me or had a grudge against me."

"I guess we'll find out in time," Griffin said. "But sometimes these things can be quite minor. It may even have been an imagined insult. Maybe she said 'good morning' one day and you didn't respond. Or you forgot her birthday or sat in her favorite chair."

"Even if one of those things *was* the trigger, I can't believe she would be guilty of killing Evan."

"Jenna Avery has proved that she is a liar. Riley and I have told Detective Iglesias about our conversation with her. Now it's up to him to find how far she would go. Is she also a murderer? Only a police investigation can uncover the truth."

Abigail got to her feet. "I'm still struggling to understand how any of this could be happening."

Just then the baby monitor kicked into life. "Does Maya need food?" Griffin asked.

"No. She's eaten lunch," Abigail said. "A drink

and some fruit will be enough to keep her going until dinner. Why?"

"Let's go out. Some fresh air will take our minds off what's going on."

Although she appreciated the suggestion, Abigail couldn't help wondering if anything would distract her from her thoughts. She was being pursued by a sinister figure who wanted to destroy her. Until today that person had been faceless. The possibility that it could be Jenna had shaken her to the core of her being. Someone she had known for so long, worked beside every day, talked to and laughed with... It made everything so much worse than if her attacker had been a stranger.

When Griffin brought Maya through from the bedroom, the baby's usual post-nap grumpiness lasted for as long as it took Abigail to change her diaper. Once she'd been placed in her high chair and given a snack of formula and stewed fruit, Maya was all smiles.

"My sisters were like that when we were kids," Griffin said. "The best way to keep them happy was to feed them. Sometimes it still is."

It was rare for him to talk about his family and, as she checked that Maya's bag was stocked with everything they needed, Abigail sent a sidelong glance in his direction. "Growing up in a house with two sets of female twins. Did that make you and Riley closer?"

"No." His expression was closed, and she thought he wasn't going to say any more, then his shoulders relaxed. "You must have guessed by now that I didn't entirely fit in."

Even though she had figured out that he felt out of place within his adoptive family, Abigail sensed that this was an area where she had to tread carefully. All the research she'd done prior to Maya's birth had told her how necessary a sense of identity was to an adopted person. It was critical that she didn't do or say anything to undermine Griffin's self-worth.

"I can see that you are very important to your siblings."

He appeared to consider her words carefully as though the idea hadn't occurred to him until now. "I think that's true. And, if you asked my brother and my sisters, I'm sure they would strenuously deny that I am not one of them."

"But?" Abigail probed gently.

"I can only speak for myself. And I have never *really* felt like a Colton."

"That must be very hard." She covered his hand with her own.

He shrugged. "There are worse things in life."

She watched his face, unsure how far to push him. Physically, this man shared so much of himself with her. When she examined her feelings for him, she knew that Griffin Colton had changed her life forever. But she was forced to hold her own emotions back because she knew he was afraid of letting go. So maybe it was time for her to take his and lead him…

"Like knowing your parent had been killed?" As soon as she'd spoken, she regretted the words. The pain that flitted across his face almost took her breath away and she reached up to touch his cheek. "I'm sorry. I shouldn't have said that."

"No. You're right. I was very lucky to have been given a home by Graham and Kathleen. I was loved and cared for. In many ways my life with them was privileged but I was also given a sense of responsibility and social justice." He caught hold of her hand, pressing it to his lips. "Even so, they didn't shape who I am."

"Your mom did that." Tears stung her eyelids at the thought of the child he'd been and the pain he'd endured.

"Everything I am is because of her."

"She would be so proud of you, Griffin." Abigail reached up and drew his face down to hers so she could kiss him lightly on the lips.

"Thank you for that."

Maya, clearly feeling she had been left out of the conversation for long enough, let out a loud belch. When it got them both to turn around, she clapped her hands.

"Oh, no." Griffin shook his head. "We are not going to start applauding bodily functions."

She gave him one of her cheeky grins and drummed her heels noisily against the high chair.

"Does that mean you want to get out?" Griffin asked.

Maya held up her arms in response. Griffin lifted her from the chair and held her up while Abigail cleaned her face and hands with baby wipes. As she did, two things occurred to her. One was how quickly they'd gotten into a baby care routine. The second was that Griffin's expression had lightened. Even though he hadn't really opened up about his childhood, she sensed that the first barrier had been breached.

As their eyes met over Maya's head, he smiled, and she knew he was letting her know that she was right.

Sheridan Park was busy with families and dog walkers. Griffin took Lucy on her harness and leash and, as usual, she attracted a mixture of reactions. Most people admired the cute little ferret, who performed a range of gymnastic tricks. Several were curious and asked questions about her. Only a few were wary and regarded the unusual animal anxiously as though she might be about to break free and go into attack mode at any minute.

Maya, watching from the comfort of her stroller, chuckled at the antics of her ferret buddy. As they strolled around the lake, Griffin was pleased that Abigail appeared relaxed and reasonably content. She'd taken the news about Jenna hard but he admired the way she dealt with everything that came her way. Lately, just when she thought things couldn't get worse, she was rocked by more bad news. Yet she faced each blow with determination and courage. Her inner strength was amazing, and he figured it must have built up when she'd had to cope alone during the difficult years of her childhood. Even though their personalities were different, they had so much in common.

"I used to come here with my mom," she said, as

they followed a path around the water's edge. "My dad was very controlling, and he didn't like her to leave the house without him, but she tried to make my life as normal as possible. We'd sneak out and spend time here, feeding the ducks and eating ice cream."

"She sounds like a remarkable woman."

"She was. Most people don't understand that because she left me behind when she finally ran out on my dad. They figure that only a very selfish woman could have done something like that to her child." Her face was half-turned away from him as if she was watching the wildfowl on the water, but he sensed her mind was focused on another time and place. "But you have to know my dad to understand the circumstances. He'd made her life a living hell and she'd reached the point where she had to leave before he broke her. She couldn't have known when she went that he would stop her from seeing me again."

"When someone is driven to take desperate action, they often can't see any alternatives," Griffin said.

"My mom was scared and in hiding. She had no money, no family and no one to help her fight him." Abigail turned to look at him. "She needed someone like you to advise her."

"Let me see if I've got the math right. You were ten when Sofia left Wes left, right? That means I was seven." He bumped her shoulder gently with his own. "I don't think I'd have been much use to your mom."

Laughing, she dug him in the ribs with her elbow. "You know what I meant."

Just as Griffin was enjoying the carefree moment,

his cell phone buzzed. Although he was tempted to ignore it, there were too many claims on his attention. His junior colleagues were all good at their jobs, but there were times when his expertise was needed. And the Colton siblings had an agreed code that they would be there for each other at all times. Then, of course, there was always the possibility that the police had news.

Sure enough, the call was from Emmanuel Iglesias. The detective didn't bother with a greeting. "I just stopped by your place." There was an urgency in his tone that concerned Griffin. "Where are you?"

"In Sheridan Park. What's this all about?"

"Are Abigail Matthews and her daughter with you?"

"Yes. But what—?"

"Go to the coffee shop at the park entrance and wait for me there. I'm on my way." The detective ended the call before Griffin could say any more.

He stared at the screen of his cell for a few seconds, his mind running through a list of possibly reasons for Emmanuel's unusual behavior. If he was coming to arrest Abigail, Griffin wouldn't let that happen. Not without a fight.

Abigail's hand on his arm drew his attention back to her. "What was that about?"

"Emmanuel Iglesias wants us to meet him at the coffee shop."

Her face paled and he could tell she was having the same thoughts as he. Had her anonymous tormentor managed to plant more evidence to convince the police of her guilt? Was Emmanuel on his way to finally slap the cuffs on her?

She swallowed hard. "Why?

"He didn't say." Gently, he placed her hand on the bar of Maya's stroller and covered it with his own. "But there's only one way to find out."

Chapter 13

To Abigail, each step that took them closer to the coffee shop at the park entrance represented the clanging of a closing prison door. Why else would Emmanuel need to see them with such urgency?

Her feet were moving in time with Griffin's, but every nerve ending was crying out for her to swing the stroller around and run in the opposite direction. The person who wanted to frame her had won. The police were coming to get her. But she couldn't be parted from her baby...and Griffin.

When they reached the entrance to the coffee shop, Griffin stopped. "We can't take Lucy inside." He looked around. "Since there's no sign of Emmanuel, we'll wait here."

There were a few people around and Abigail's attention was instantly drawn to a small, slight figure dressed all in black. It was such a warm day, and it seemed odd that anyone would wear a sweatshirt with the hood pulled up. As the person moved toward them, she noticed that he, or she, was also wearing shades.

At the last minute, she saw the outstretched hand and the knife pointed directly at Maya. Her throat tightened with dread. When she tried to cry out and let Griffin know what was happening, no sound came out. With only a split second to act, she threw herself between the lethal weapon and her baby.

Time slowed. Heat seared Abigail's upper left arm as the knife sliced through her flesh. The stroller tilted and she tumbled with it to the ground. Scrambling desperately to protect Maya, she lay over the top of the stroller and anticipated the next slice of the blade.

As if from a distance, Griffin shouted, and Maya started to cry. When Abigail looked up, the hooded attacker was standing over her holding the bloodied blade inches from her face. As she lifted her right hand to shield her face, a tiny, furry figure darted out from beneath the stroller. Lucy sank her sharp teeth into the assailant's left wrist at the top of the gloved hand that held the knife.

Letting out a screech, the hooded figure dropped the weapon and tried to shake Lucy free. With her leash hanging loose, the little ferret hung on tight.

Pain washed over Abigail. Warm blood was pouring down her arm and her vision started to fade. Desperately clinging to consciousness, she tried to look around to see if Maya was okay. Unsure whether the pounding in her ears was her own heartbeat or running footsteps, she was relieved to hear Emmanuel call out a warning.

"GRPD. Stay right where you are."

Ignoring him, the attacker finally knocked Lucy away and spun around. Although Abigail couldn't see what was going on, she heard the detective talking into his radio. "Sheridan Park. Close down the exits. The suspect is on foot and moving fast. She's injured and leaving a trail of blood."

She?

Griffin was kneeling beside her, but his face was an indistinct blur as he removed his T-shirt and used it to apply pressure to her injury. "We need paramedics here. Fast. She's been stabbed."

"Maya?" She clutched his wrist with her right hand.

He slid an arm around her, and she rested her head against his shoulder. "She's unhurt. Detective Lopez has her. We'll take her to the hospital with us."

"What about Lucy?" She managed to gasp out the question. "She saved my life."

"Emmanuel doesn't know it yet but he's about to take a ferret into protective custody."

When he joined them, Emmanuel was carrying Maya and holding Lucy's leash. "The paramedics are on their way." As if to confirm the truth of his statement, they heard the sound of approaching sirens. "Uh. What do you want me to do with the rodent?"

"Get someone to take her to my sister, Sadie. She'll

look after her until I can collect her," Griffin said. He took Maya from Emmanuel and, although the baby tucked her head into his neck, Abigail was pleased to see that her tears had subsided. "Then, you need to explain what's going on."

"Yeah." Emmanuel nodded. "After I've coordinated the search and taken care of the wildlife, I'll follow you to the hospital."

Detective Lopez had done a good job of keeping any onlookers back and the ambulance was able to drive right up to the steps of the coffee shop. As it stopped, Emmanuel started to walk away.

"Wait." Abigail's voice was a croak. Shock was setting in. She was shivering wildly, and her teeth chattered as though she was freezing. But she had to know *now*. Later wouldn't do. "You said the person who attacked me was a she. Does that mean you know who it was?"

"Yes." His expression was grim. "It was Jenna Avery."

Once they were in the ambulance and on the way to the hospital, two paramedics examined Abigail. Griffin's anxiety for her was off the scale, but he maintained a calm exterior for Maya's sake. Although the baby had recovered from the shock of having her stroller overturned, she had picked up the tension in the atmosphere and was clingy and whiny.

The paramedics had guided him to a seat that was out of the way of the action and requested that he fasten himself and Maya in so that they were safe during the ride. It meant Maya couldn't see her mom and she kept up a loud protest throughout the journey.

"It's okay. I'm here," Griffin told her. She gave him a tear-stained look that told him that, right at that moment, he wasn't what she wanted.

It wasn't easy to hear what the paramedics were saying while he was trying to comfort the distressed baby, but he strained to listen to their conversation. "Vital signs are all okay, but the wound is deep and she's lost a lot of blood."

"I'm calling ahead. We need the trauma team prepped and ready for surgery."

Surgery. What did that mean, exactly? Could Abigail lose the use of that arm? Was amputation a possibility? *Tell me she's not going to die...*

When they reached the hospital, there was an emergency team waiting for them. Griffin caught only a brief glimpse of Abigail's face as they rolled the gurney past him and into the building. She wasn't conscious. Her beautiful features were as pale and still as a marble statue. Her T-shirt was stained a deep crimson.

"She's lost so much blood. Will she be okay?" He unfastened himself and Maya and got to his feet.

"If you follow the signs to the family room, sir, someone will be with you as soon as they can." It wasn't an answer.

Tuning into his mood, Maya hooked a hand behind his neck and rested her cheek against his chest. For an instant, he battled to keep control of his emotions. Holding Maya firmly, he walked into the building.

The family room was small and cozy with bright pictures on the walls and a well-stocked toy corner. There was no one else around and, after sitting Maya on the rug with some play items, Griffin took his cell phone out of his pocket. There were messages from all his siblings. One of Emmanuel's colleagues had taken Lucy to Sadie's place and, while handing over the ferret, had given her a brief account of what had happened to Abigail. The family support system had already swung into action. For the first time in his life, Griffin felt like a Colton.

On our way. Riley's text was brief, to the point. And very welcome.

He knelt on the floor beside Maya, trying to distract himself by playing with her, but his whole body hurt. He couldn't get enough air into his lungs and his heart felt as if it was trying to burst out of his chest. Even as he talked to Maya about the toys, his brain was asking "what if?"

Panic was like an iron fist tightening its grip on his gut. This couldn't be happening. He couldn't have found Abigail only to lose her this way. When he thought back to all those doubts he'd had about her and how hurt she must have been… He clenched a fist on his thigh. That was in the past. They'd moved on. Even so, what if she died without knowing how much he cared?

Although he was alone in the darkness of his thoughts for less than half an hour, it felt like forever. When Riley and Charlize finally dashed into the room, he felt the first burn of tears at the back of his eyelids and blinked hard. He needed to be strong for Maya. And Abigail...

"Oh, my goodness." Charlize fell to her knees beside Griffin, wrapping her arms around him. "How are you holding up?"

He drew in a shaky breath. "I'd be a lot better if I knew what was going on."

"You mean no one has told you anything?" Riley looked around at the empty room.

Griffin got to his feet, leaving Charlize and Maya playing together. "I figure they need to be with Abigail, not out here talking to me."

"Even so, you must be out of your mind with worry. Why don't we stay here with Maya while you see if you can find someone who can tell you what's happening?"

When Griffin tried to thank him, his voice refused to work and the only sound that emerged was a grunt. He saw the understanding in his brother's eyes as Riley placed a hand on his shoulder and steered him toward the door. When he left the room, he noticed a sign directing him to the reception desk. Before he began to follow it, a female doctor approached him.

"Are you here with Dr. Matthews?"

There it was again. That tightness in his throat that made it hard to talk. "Yes."

Suddenly, he wanted to walk away and not hear what this woman had to say. Right now, everything was okay. She could change that with a few words.

"Please follow me." She led him along a corridor

and into a small office. "May I ask what your relationship is to Dr. Matthews?"

It was a tricky question and one to which he didn't know the answer. Since this was not the time or place for soul-searching, he decided to be as honest as he needed to be. "We live together."

She seemed satisfied with that. "Okay. I'm Dr. Reynolds. I led the surgical team who operated on Dr. Matthews. We had to stabilize her condition and reduce the bleeding before we could treat her injury. Because of the severity of the wound, we administered a general anesthetic to determine the extent of the damage. Although there was significant trauma caused by the blade penetration, I'm hopeful that there will be no long-term effects to her arm. The greater concern was dealing with the amount of blood Dr. Matthews lost."

"What treatment has she been given?" Griffin asked.

"After cleansing the wound, we closed it using sutures. We are administering intravenous fluids and antibiotics and she has been given a blood transfusion. It's possible she may need more blood but that's something we'll judge when she comes around from the anesthetic. We'll continue to monitor her vital signs, of course and, longer term, she'll need physiotherapy."

"But she will recover?"

She placed a hand on his arm. "Yes. I have every confidence that she will make a full recovery."

He bowed his head, the relief that flooded through

him almost as overwhelming as the fear it replaced. Abigail was alive and she would be okay. "Can I see her?"

"Yes. She's awake now and has already asked for both you and someone called Maya."

"That's our daughter." He said the words without thinking but as soon as he heard the phrase out loud it made him pause. *Our daughter.* Two little words that contained everything he wanted for the future. "Can I take her to see Abigail?"

"Of course. You can see her together."

When she first came around from the anesthetic, Abigail felt like she'd been sleeping for too long and too deeply. Now, she was tired but impatient to see Griffin and Maya. Obediently following the nurse's instructions to rest, she had her eyes closed when she heard Maya let out a cry of delight as they entered the room.

"Yes, it's your mom." Griffin was talking softly. "But we need to be quiet so we don't disturb her."

"I'm awake." Even though she'd been conscious for some time, there was still a slight slurring to her words, as if she was tipsy.

Griffin was at her side instantly. "I'll call the nurse."

"No. I'm fine. She said to use the call button if I need anything." She turned her head slightly so she could look at him and Maya. "This is nice. Just us."

"How do you feel?" He shook his head. "Stupid question."

She lifted her right hand and touched his wrist before stroking Maya's cheek. "Jenna ran away. Did they catch her?"

"No." The voice came from the doorway as, with perfect timing, Emmanuel strode into the room. "I'm sorry I don't have better news for you, but she mingled with the crowds in the park and we lost her. We're still searching, of course."

"I've been waiting for you to tell us exactly what's going on," Griffin said.

"Are you strong enough to have this conversation now?" Emmanuel asked Abigail.

"I need to know why I'm in this hospital bed." She tried to shift position and winced as pain shot through her injured arm. "And whether I have to worry about the future."

"Okay." Emmanuel pulled up a visitor's chair and indicated for Griffin to do the same. When Griffin was seated, Maya settled onto his knee and, by the way her eyelids were drooping, it looked as if she would soon be asleep. "I followed up the information from Griffin and Riley about Jenna's dishonesty over the RevitaYou pills and paid her a visit. When I interviewed her, she came across as very edgy. There wasn't anything specific, but I got the definite impression that she was hiding something. After I left her apartment, I decided to hang around and watch the place. Sure enough, ten minutes later, she came hurrying out carrying a large travel bag. She got into her car and drove off like the hounds of hell were chasing her."

"Did you follow her?" Griffin asked.

"I tried but I lost her after a few blocks. We didn't have enough evidence to get a search warrant for her home address but, after Dr. Hardin's murder, I was able to search Jenna's office at Danvers University. She hadn't been very careful about covering up her obsession with you, Abigail."

"Obsession?" Abigail reached out her right hand and Griffin took hold of it.

"In one drawer of her desk, she had a file containing pictures and cuttings from academic texts. It must have contained everything that was ever printed about you," Emmanuel said.

"But why?" Abigail asked. "We were friends."

"Not according to this." Emmanuel withdrew a book from the inside pocket of his jacket. Although it was contained within an evidence bag, Abigail could see that it looked like a journal of some kind. "This is Jenna's diary. In it, she helpfully documents how she added Anthrosyne to the Mem10 trial and tried to frame you for it. How she wanted to further ruin your reputation by pretending to have taken Revita-You and gotten ill. She goes into detail about how she killed Evan Hardin because he was about to fire her from her job but how she callously used his death as another chance to get back at you. And, as I already said, she outlined her plans to kill you and Maya, if the police get close to her."

"Get back at me?" Abigail couldn't manage to raise her voice above a whisper. "For what?"

"She has always been jealous of you, both personally and professionally. There is a lot of ranting in the diary about your looks and how you rose to your current position at the university. But she seems to have become unhinged recently because she believes you were investigating her role in an online adoption scam."

Griffin sat up a little straighter and Maya gave a sleepy grumble. "So she *was* living a double life as Anne Jay?"

"I don't understand." Abigail looked from one man to the other in confusion.

"I didn't have time to talk to you about my suspicions," Griffin explained. "But one of my cases involved an online adoption scam. The woman at the heart of it looked a lot like Jenna. From what Emmanuel is saying, it appears it *was* her."

"It was," Emmanuel confirmed. "Jenna had been conning childless couples in an online adoption fraud for several years. Basically, she used the miscarriage project you were both involved in to target childless couples. She targeted them through social media, introducing herself as the head of Morning-Star Families, a private, online adoption agency. After building up a relationship with the vulnerable person, or couple, she would 'introduce' them to the pregnant woman who was supposedly carrying their child and ask for money for expenses. Over the course of the so-called pregnancy, photographs and documents would be exchanged as well as cash. The pregnant woman didn't exist, of course, and when the nine months were over, Jenna simply ceased all contact with the couple who had been paying her."

"But that's awful." Abigail was horrified.

"Preying on people when they were at their most vulnerable is something that I see too often," Griffin said. "And social media allows people like Jenna to do it anonymously."

"But she knew someone was on to her. Her social media accounts were being tracked and someone was making inquiries about MorningStar Families," Emmanuel said. "You, Abigail, had been talking openly about your research into adoption. Jenna put the two things together and became convinced that you had discovered her guilty secret. She lied about RevitaYou to make you look bad. When Evan called her into his office and told her she was fired, she was certain you had reported your findings to him. The truth was that she'd been falsifying records again. He'd covered up for her in the past because they'd had a brief affair and she was using it to blackmail him but this time she'd gone too far. The details were all on his computer. It looks like she killed him before he had time to explain because she continued to blame you."

"*I* was the person who was on to her." Griffin lightly squeezed Abigail's hand. "When I think what could have happened…"

He looked torn apart with tiredness and worry. She returned his grip. "Hey. I'm still here."

"We need to talk about that," Emmanuel said. "I hate to do this right now, but Jenna is still on the loose and she's sworn to kill you and Maya."

* * *

Griffin's fears were back, only this time they were stronger than ever. Jenna Avery was unhinged, and she wanted to harm his new family. And no one knew where she was, or when she would strike.

"How are you going to look after them?" he asked Emmanuel.

"While Abigail is in the hospital, we'll put a guard on this room," the police officer said. "Detective Lopez is in the family room with your brother and his fiancée. He can take the first shift."

"But what about Maya?" Abigail's face, already pale, turned ashen as she looked at the baby, who was now sleeping in Griffin's arms. "Jenna's threat was directed at both of us."

"I won't let her out of my sight," Griffin promised.

Tears brimmed in her eyes. "I can't bear this. How can I lie helpless in this bed, knowing that Jenna is out there just waiting to snatch my baby and harm her?"

Griffin knew exactly what she meant. He also knew it wouldn't do her recovery any good to be separated from her daughter at a time like this. Abigail would be distraught with worry every second she and Maya were apart.

"I need to talk to the doctor." Easing Maya into the crook of his arm, he got to his feet. "You'll be here with Abigail the whole time I'm gone, right?" He asked Emmanuel.

The detective nodded. "You can count on it."

Still carrying Maya, Griffin returned to the family room. Riley and Charlize were deep in conversation with Daniel Lopez and he figured that Emmanuel's partner had given them all the details about Jenna and her obsession with Abigail. All three of them looked up when he entered.

"How is Abigail?" Riley asked.

"She's going to be okay." He still felt the weight of everything those words meant about his feelings and his hopes for the future. "I have to go find the doctor and then I have something I need to run by you."

"Anything we can do to help." Riley placed a hand on his shoulder. "You know that."

"Let me take Maya." Charlize was on her feet in an instant, and he carefully handed the sleeping baby over.

"I guess you know about the threats from Jenna Avery?" Griffin spoke directly to Daniel Lopez.

"Don't worry." The detective nodded. "I'll be right here with your baby."

"Thank you."

When he reached the reception desk and asked for Dr. Reynolds, Griffin expected he would have a long wait. She was an emergency surgeon, after all. He was surprised when she joined him after a few minutes.

"My shift is just ending," she explained as they walked into her tiny office. "How can I help you?"

Quickly, he outlined the situation. "While I understand that Abigail may need recovery time in the hospital, I'm concerned about the effects on her well-being if she is separated from her daughter at such a difficult time."

The doctor frowned. "What are you proposing as an alternative?"

"If Abigail can be moved to my brother's home in Heritage Hill, my siblings and I will be able to take full-time responsibility for her care. She would be with Maya, and the police would have them both in one place, so their protection would be simpler. Her caseworker will need to agree to this arrangement as well, of course."

Dr. Reynolds was silent for a few moments. "I had envisaged Dr. Matthews being hospitalized for at least a few days. Since the circumstances are unusual, I'm prepared to consider your suggestion on the condition that we arrange for a nurse to visit her each day. And, if she shows any sign of a temperature, sickness, or the wound appears to be infected, then she must return to hospital immediately."

"Of course. I won't do anything to put her in danger," Griffin assured her. "All I want to do is protect her."

"I can see that." The doctor smiled for the first time. "She's a very lucky lady."

"After everything that's happened to her recently, I'm not sure she'd agree with you."

He returned to the family room and shared the details of his plan with Riley, who immediately started making plans. As Griffin listened to his brother making calls to the other siblings, alerting them to the situation and enlisting their help to get a room ready for Abigail at the CI headquarters, his heart expanded with warmth. This was his family and now they were opening their arms to Abigail and Maya the same way they had accepted him all those years ago.

"How about we take Maya home with us now?" Riley asked when he finished his calls. He turned to Detective Lopez. "Does your vehicle have a car seat?"

"No, but I can get one here within minutes that does." He started talking into his radio.

"What about your vehicle?" Griffin asked.

Riley flapped a hand. "Details. We can sort that out tomorrow."

Griffin briefly gripped his arm in a gesture of gratitude. "Thank you."

"Hey. Maya will have a little cousin soon enough." There it was. That assumption that Maya's place in their lives was permanent. Griffin only hoped Riley was right. "I know you'd do the same for us if the time came."

They spent the next few minutes getting the sleeping baby out to the parking lot and into the patrol car that had pulled up outside the front entrance of the building. Detective Lopez got in the driver's seat with Riley next to him. Charlize sat next to Maya in the rear.

Before the police officer drove away, Griffin leaned into the window to speak to him. "What are the chances that Jenna Avery could be watching the hospital?"

"It's a possibility."

"Could she follow you? Or the ambulance that takes Jenna to the CI headquarters?"

"If she does, we'll be ready for her." The detective's lips thinned into a line. "But don't build her up into something she's not. She's a woman on the run and, thanks to your weird pet, she's also injured."

For now, Griffin figured that was the best he could hope for. He stepped back, watching the vehicle as it drove away. A quick scan of the area outside the hospital showed nothing suspicious and, reassured that the police were protecting Abigail and Maya, he went back inside.

Chapter 14

By the time the ambulance reached the CI headquarters, Abigail was exhausted and aching all over. But she wasn't going to complain. This solution of Griffin's meant she could heal in a safe place among people she knew. And the best part was that she didn't have to be parted from Maya.

When the emergency vehicle pulled up at the rear of the house, two orderlies carefully pushed her wheelchair into the building.

"I can walk," Abigail protested. "My arm is in a sling, but my legs work just fine."

"I don't know." One of them regarded her dubiously. "The doctor told us to use our judgment and you do look pale."

"How about she takes my arm?" Griffin said. "That way she can lean on me?"

The orderlies appeared to feel that was an acceptable compromise. As Griffin helped her from the wheelchair, and her legs trembled, she realized just how weak she was. When she finally stepped into the house, she felt like she'd just run a marathon.

"Where's Maya?" she asked.

"She's having dinner with my sisters." He pointed in the direction of the dining room. "Do you want to go through there and join them, or shall I take you to your bedroom so you can rest?"

She smiled. "I want to see Maya, of course."

He gave an exaggerated sigh. "Sure you do. Even though the doctor told me to make sure you got plenty of rest."

They walked slowly to the room where the entire Colton family were gathered around the table. Exclamations of delight greeted Abigail's arrival, and Griffin escorted her to a chair next to Maya's high chair. The baby cooed with pleasure and offered her mom a mangled piece of toast.

"It's okay, honey. The doctor advised against pre-chewed food at this stage of my recovery."

"It's so good to see you." Kiely reached across the table and pressed her uninjured hand. "What a terrible ordeal."

"The hero ferret can stay at my place as long as she needs to," Sadie said. "I borrowed an old cage from a neighbor whose dog had pups recently, so she's secure and I stopped by Griffin's place to pick up her toys and food."

Abigail was struck again by the genuine niceness of these people. They were investigating her dad, so they knew exactly what he'd done, and there was a time when they'd believed she was part of his schemes. Even if that was no longer the case, they could be forgiven for believing that Wes Matthews's daughter was no good. Raised by a crook, she might have turned out to be every bit as bad as her father.

But they'd been prepared to believe in her. Although she knew part of that was for Griffin's sake, it felt good that they'd been open enough to judge her on who she was rather than on her notorious relative. And now, as Sadie pressed her to have a hot drink and Vikki asked if she was too warm, she felt like she'd been part of this group forever. This was what a family felt like. How wonderful that she was able to experience it for herself.

Tiredness settled over her and she let the conversation continue around her without attempting to be part of it. The siblings were discussing the police protection for her and Maya and whether they also needed to employ private bodyguards.

"While my instinct is to get an army and surround the place, we have to consider what Detective Lopez said." Was it her imagination, or did Griffin seem more comfortable in his place at the table than he had on the other occasions she'd seen him there? "We can't build the threat from Jenna out of proportion. She's a lone woman on the run and Lucy gave her a hell of a bite. She has to be hurting badly. Possibly that wound is even infected. Even if she tries to carry out her threat, she's up against all of us and the police."

He looked around the table and Abigail could see him checking whether he had the agreement of the other members of the family.

"I'm not prepared to put Abigail and Maya at risk, so we have to be extra vigilant. But Riley, Charlize and I will be here full-time. In addition, Emmanuel is putting a police guard on the house 24/7. Plus the rest of you will be checking in regularly. Between us, I think we will be able to keep them safe until the police have Jenna in custody." He turned to Abigail and the smile in his eyes drove her weariness away. "The final decision has to be yours."

"I feel safe with you." After a few seconds, she remembered that they weren't alone. "All of you."

"Then that's settled. But we'll keep reviewing the situation and, if necessary, we can bring in additional security."

There was some general conversation, then Pippa let out a little cry.

"What is it? What's wrong?" Sadie asked.

"It's a text from Brody." Pippa held up her cell phone so they could see the display. "It just came through a second ago."

"I guess it makes sense he would contact you," Riley said. "Out of all of us, you are the one he has always been closest to."

"He's still in hiding." Pippa read the message to

them. "He's terrified and desperate to know if Wes Matthews has been caught yet. He knows that's the only way he'll get his money back and be able to pay Capital X so he can come out of hiding and stop living in fear."

There were gloomy faces around the table and Abigail bowed her head.

"I hate to give Brody bad news when things are going so badly for him, but I'll have to reply and tell him that Wes is still on the run," Pippa said. "The only hope I can offer him is that we're working on it round the clock."

"Wait." Griffin stopped her before she could start typing out her response. "Maybe we should just pay back Capital X for Brody so he can come out of hiding?"

There was a stunned silence around the table and Abigail remembered the way Griffin had spoken about Brody when they'd first met. She'd gotten the impression that his feelings toward Brody were complicated. Clearly, she'd been right.

"Would you do that for Brody? And do we even have that kind of liquid cash?" Pippa asked.

"He doesn't deserve what's happening to him," Griffin said. "No one does."

"I'll text him back right away and tell him that we'll pay off his debt to Capital X." Pippa sent the reply and set her cell phone down on the table. There was an expectant hush in the room, but nothing happened. When there was no reply after a few minutes, the tension level wound down a little.

"It looks like Brody's gone silent again," Kiely said.

"Maybe he's had to start running again?" Sadie suggested.

"Or he could be too proud to let us pay his debt," Vikki said.

Griffin moved around the table to sit next to Abigail, checking that she was okay. "Which do you think it is?" She spoke quietly so that only he could hear. "Is he on the run again, or is he too proud?"

"I don't know." He lifted Maya from her high chair and held her on his lap, making sure that the baby could touch Abigail without hurting her. "But if Brody has gone quiet because it would hurt his pride if we paid to help him out of this situation… Well, it would make me think a lot more kindly of him than I've done in the past."

She studied his face. "Was that hard for you to say?"

He shrugged. "Not as hard as it would once have been. Brody found life easy. I found it hard. For a long time, I struggled to accept that it was because we're different people not because my family treated us any differently."

She placed her uninjured hand over his. "You're a good man, Griffin."

He smiled. "You're just saying that because you know you need my help. You can't change a diaper one-handed."

That night, Griffin shared a room with Maya, while Abigail slept in the first-floor room that Charlize had prepared specially for her. Despite the painkillers, she had a restless night. The following morning, Griffin persuaded her to rest for most of the morning while he took care of Maya. When she finally insisted on getting out of bed, she asked him to send Charlize to help her shower.

"I can do that," he said. "Riley and Maya are playing with Pal in the hall."

She gave him a stern look. "Griffin, I will be more than happy to share a shower with you when my arm is mended. But you are not going to be my nurse."

He slid an arm around her waist and drew her close. "I want to take care of you."

"You do." She rubbed her cheek against his chest. "And I—" She stopped and hitched in a breath. "Couldn't manage without you."

"That's not what you were going to say."

"No, it's not." She tilted her head back and smiled up at him. "But there's a time and a place for everything. And this time and place are for me to shower and for you to make me lunch."

She gave him a playful shove toward the door with her right hand. As he followed her instructions and started to prepare lunch, Griffin wondered what she *had* almost said. *And I...what? "And I love you?"* Was that too much to hope for? There were times when he didn't think it was. He knew she cared for him. The closeness they shared didn't need words. But he wasn't sure about what she wanted for the long term. And that terrified him.

Because he knew exactly what he wanted. He wanted Abigail. And Maya. He wanted his little family. Forever. The prospect of a future without them in it was bleak and unbearable.

To distract himself, he turned on the TV and flicked through the news channels, pausing when a familiar item caught his attention. The anchor was holding up a bottle of RevitaYou pills. Griffin stopped chopping vegetables for a salad and turned up the sound.

"The woman, who has not yet been named, died in Grand Rapids Hospital in the early hours of this morning. Her death has been linked to the controversial supplement RevitaYou. Extensive testing on the unregulated vitamins has revealed that the formula is toxic and potentially fatal. Since no one can be sure who will be affected, the public are being advised not take this product and to dispose of any unused pills."

"Oh, no."

Griffin turned to see Abigail standing in the kitchen doorway, holding on to the frame with her good hand as she stared at the TV. Her hair was damp and piled up on top of her head in a loose knot and she wore sweatpants and a T-shirt. He hurried to her side, sliding an arm around her waist to support her. She leaned against him, resting her head on his shoulder.

"I knew it was only a matter of time before someone died." Her voice trembled with emotion. "The ricin in those pills means the people taking them are dicing with death. But now my dad is a killer as well as a con man."

"Will people listen to the warning?" Griffin wondered. "When we put out social media blasts about

RevitaYou causing sickness, there were always those who fired back at us about how much they loved the vitamins."

"Let's see what the response to the news of the death has been." Abigail fumbled her cell out of her jeans pocket with her good hand. Griffin looked over her shoulder as she checked the RevitaYou hashtag. "Look at this." She shook her head, her expression disbelieving. "People are still defending RevitaYou, calling it a wonder drug. There are dozens who are claiming it's made them look twenty-nine instead of forty-five."

Griffin pointed out one post. I'd rather die than be an old hag. "I'm sure it's meant as a joke, but it's not exactly good taste on a day like this."

"I don't usually reply, but I can't let that pass." Abigail awkwardly used one hand to hold her phone and type her reply. This is no joke. Someone has died. "And I know more deaths are coming. What will it take to stop people from taking these hateful, poisonous 'vitamins'?"

"The only way I can see this ending is if there *are* more deaths," Griffin said. "People have to take notice if they think they could die as a result of trying to look younger."

"You read some of those posts." Abigail looked seriously worried. "I genuinely think there are some who would take a chance."

"Then we have to keep trying to lure your dad and Landon Street out of hiding. A court case is the only other way to highlight the dangers." He ran a hand through his hair. "But I know how much you hate the idea of being drawn into that."

"I hate the idea of even more people dying."

"Do you think you can eat some lunch?" he asked.

She gave him a weak smile. "Are you asking because the doctor told you to take good care of me?"

"The nurse is coming this afternoon. We have to be able to tell her what a model patient you are."

She huffed out a mock sigh. "In that case, I guess I could manage a little lunch."

"There's a good patient." He guided her toward the dining room. "Oh, and Abigail?"

"Yes, Griffin?"

"I would take good care of you, whether a doctor told me to or not."

"I know you would." He caught a glimmer of tears in her eyes and wanted to lighten the mood. She was right when she said there was a time and a place for the deep conversations. The devastating news about the RevitaYou death had already taken its toll on her emotions. He didn't want any more setbacks.

"I have to." He leaned closer to whisper in her ear. "You promised me that, when you're well again, we get to share a shower."

The nurse had finished cleaning and dressing Abigail's wound. She had left, giving her strict instructions not to overdo things before she returned the following day. Abigail lay back on her pillows feeling tired, slightly nauseated and tearful. Those emotions had been her companions almost constantly since she'd left the hospital.

What is the matter with me?

She tapped a finger to her chin. *Let me see.*

Could it be the fact that my former friend, not content with having stabbed me, wants to kill me and my little girl? Or that I had surgery yesterday to repair the five-inch wound in my arm? Or that I have to stay hidden away like a fugitive with a patrol car at the gates? Or is it maybe that my dad has finally upgraded from fraudster to killer?

That was before she started on the other things: someone had killed her boss, her professional reputation was in shreds, the fate of the research of which she was so proud hung in the balance, people hated her because of her name...

There were so many reasons for her to feel low, it was impossible to single out just one. And yet, if she was honest, she wasn't sure if any of those were responsible for this weight pressing down on her. Her mood ricocheted between low and lower and she couldn't summon the inner strength on which she'd always relied in times of trouble.

Part of her mind kept dwelling on this house. On the Colton family. And on Griffin. What was she ever going to do when they were no longer part of her life? She gave a soft, bitter laugh.

They? *You mean "he."*

The Coltons were very special people. They'd made her feel like part of their family. But she was in love with Griffin, not his siblings.

She loved him, and she was certain that he loved her. Could he ever acknowledge that or admit it? His traumatic early life had left him with emotional scars that were so deep he might never recover. When they first met, she'd thought he was cold and distant. Now, she knew better. Behind that facade, there was a scared, shy little boy.

Being ripped out of his home and relocated at such a young age had damaged his sense of identity and had a devastating effect on his ability to form bonds. Added to that, it was clear that he had been unable to fully fit in with his Colton family. No wonder he was afraid of getting too close to another person, scared of letting his craving for love show.

But, whether he liked it or not, they were in a relationship. Despite all the chaos around them, Griffin, Abigail, Maya and a heroic little ferret had become a family. And she was not going to give that up. Not without a fight.

There it was. She'd found her fighting spirit. Almost without noticing, the gloom had lifted from her shoulders a little and, instead of wanting to cry, she felt more like her old self. Ready to square her shoulders—well, maybe to just square one shoulder for the time being—and face the world.

Her cell phone pinged with an incoming text from an unknown number and she frowned as a photograph unfolded on the screen. It was an image of herself, clearly taken at the gym without her knowledge. She recognized the locker room decor behind her, and, in the picture, she was holding a towel against her chest as she emerged from the shower. It felt intrusive and Abigail had no memory of it being taken.

After she'd studied it for a few seconds, a message followed.

I have others. You and the Coltons love social media. Let's see how much you enjoy it when naked pictures of Wes Matthews's daughter start going viral.

There was a knock on the door and her voice shook as she called out, "Come in."

"Ready for some company?" Griffin opened the door and stepped inside. He was carrying Maya, who gave Abigail a beaming smile and held out her arms. He took one look at her face and crossed the room in quick strides. "What's happened?"

Wordlessly, she held out her cell. His face darkened with anger as he read the message. When he finished, he looked up. "Jenna?"

"It has to be. We were members of the same gym. We went together a few times. But I had no idea she was taking pictures of me."

"Forward this to Emmanuel," Griffin said. "I know she's not using her own number, but he may be able to do something."

As they were talking, Maya started squirming to get to Abigail.

"It's okay. Put her on the bed," Abigail said. "I'm not going to let Jenna spoil our time together."

Griffin came to sit next to her and placed Maya between them. The baby curled up contentedly against

Abigail's side and she drew her into the crook of her uninjured elbow for a closer snuggle. Griffin placed his arm around Abigail's shoulder, resting his cheek on her hair and they sat that way for long, silent minutes.

"This," Griffin said at last.

"I know."

"Do you?"

She held her breath for a second or two. "I love you, Griffin."

When he didn't answer, she thought she'd blown it. Closing her eyes, she blinked away the tears. Even if he never admitted it she knew he loved her. And she wouldn't regret saying it. He needed to hear it...

"I love you, too." She looked up and saw the raw emotion in his eyes. The wetness on his cheeks. "I was waiting for the right time to tell you."

She turned awkwardly, reaching over Maya's head to touch his cheek. "It's always the right time."

He nodded, leaning closer to kiss her. "Then I'll keep saying it."

Chapter 15

Griffin had the strangest feeling. As if his past, while not exactly floating away into obscurity, had at last been relegated to where it should be. It was behind him. He couldn't change what had happened and he had to move on. He had a future now.

Happiness flowed through him, warming his skin like the rays of the early morning sun. His usual cautious smile had been replaced by a grin so wide it was in danger of splitting his face in two. He would never fear love again, because he had found it. And, after all his years of angst, it had been the most natural, wonderful thing in the world.

Now, we just have to defeat the bad guys, get Maya's adoption back on track, and get on with our lives.

With that in mind, he had checked in with Emmanuel about Jenna's message to Abigail. The detective wasn't hopeful about tracing her from it.

"She's using a burner phone. The likelihood is she'll discard that one and buy another to send the next message. The chances of tracking her down that way are slim, if not nonexistent."

It was frustrating but not unexpected. Emmanuel had continued to assure him that they were doing all they could to find Jenna.

Now, still on the subject of bad guys, the CI team was gathered for another meeting. This time, the focus was on Capital X, the anonymous, underground loan company.

CI had been determined to break open Capital X. But, no matter how hard they tried to get details on the group, it was intricate and underground. Operating out of the dark web, it was as devious as it was dangerous.

The team was joined by Ashanti Silver, their brilliant technical expert.

Occasionally, a burst of laughter from the kitchen reached them and lightened the mood. Charlize was preparing dinner and Abigail had joined her, since she knew nothing about Capital X. Maya was with them and was clearly proving to be a source of entertainment. Griffin was pleased that the two women got along so well and that Maya would soon have someone in the family to play with.

"I don't have any more news for you guys about Capital X," Ashanti said. "Because they use the dark web, they are able to hide their activities well. It's a haven for bad guys."

"Explain to us again how that works," Kiely said.

"Putting it simply, imagine that the internet is a forest and within it there are well-worn paths, the ones that most people use. Those paths are the popular search engines. Away from these paths—or search engines—the trees will mask your vision. Then it becomes almost impossible to find anything, unless you know what you're looking for. This is how the dark web works, and it is essentially the name given to all the hidden places on the internet."

"So you stumble around and get lost?" Sadie said.

"Yes." Ashanti nodded. "Or you need a guide. Just like the forest, the dark web hides things well. It hides actions and it hides identities. The dark web also prevents people from knowing who you are, what you are doing and where you are doing it."

"How do you ever find your way?" Vikki asked.

Ashanti gave a confident grin. "You have to understand the forest better than everyone else."

"If the only way to communicate with Capital X is via the dark web, we have to send them a message that will make them take notice," Pippa said.

She had a reckless look about her that worried Griffin. "What do you have in mind?"

She leaned forward. "Let's take this fight to them. I think one of us should infiltrate Capital X by pretending to be looking for a big loan. They won't be able resist getting hold of another victim."

"I don't like the sound of that." Riley shook his head. "These guys are ruthless."

"Who are you suggesting should be the one to go undercover and get inside Capital X?" Griffin asked. He had a feeling he already knew the answer.

"I'll do it." Pippa tossed her head. "It's my plan, I'll be the one to see it through."

There was a general chorus of dissent, with none of the siblings approving of her suggestion. Each of Pippa's brothers and sisters had their own forceful argument to put forward for why it would be too dangerous. Pippa remained calm in the face of their opposition.

"Putting my neck out is my job. This is what I do," she insisted, when everyone was all talked out. "These low-lifes will take one look at me and think they've got their claws into another vulnerable person. They won't know I can handle myself."

"We can't let you do this," Griffin insisted. "Look at what's happened to Brody. That has to be a warning to anyone thinking of tangling with Capital X and their thugs."

She sighed. "At least let me do some more research before you try and stop me. Then I'll come back to you with a detailed plan. Ashanti, we can work together and use the dark web to find out more, right?"

Ashanti nodded. "Yeah. But stick with me. Your team are right to be nervous. These guys don't mess around."

Pippa grinned. "Nor do I."

Once the meeting was finished, Charlize served dinner to the team. Ashanti had left, having explained that she was going on a date with the love of her life, her math teacher husband, Jeffrey.

"That's so sweet." Sadie placed a hand over her heart after Ashanti had gone. "I hope Tate and I are still like that after a few years of marriage."

Abigail had noticed before how a curious silence descended whenever Sadie mentioned her fiancé, Tate Greer. It happened again now. No one responded to the comment, and the other siblings suddenly became engrossed in passing around the food and handing out drinks.

Sadie tossed her head. "Since we're all together, it seems like a good time to let you know that Tate and I have decided on a Christmas wedding."

None of the usual outpouring of congratulations followed the announcement. Abigail caught a glimpse of tears in Sadie's eyes and felt sorry for her. She didn't understand what was going on. The Coltons were such a close, caring family. How could they ignore something so important to their sister?

"Could you pass the potatoes, please?" Vikki asked Kiely.

"Don't all rush to congratulate me, will you?" Sadie's lower lip trembled as she looked around at her brothers and sisters.

"All we want is for you to be happy." Griffin reached over and pressed his sister's hand.

"But you don't think that will happen if I marry Tate." Sadie was clearly upset. Getting to her feet, she snatched up her purse with a trembling hand.

"I'm sorry, Charlize. I know you've gone to a lot of trouble, but I'm just not hungry."

Pushing back her chair, she ran from the room. Her heels clattered on the kitchen floor and they heard the rear door slam behind her.

"I'll go after her." Riley followed her from the room.

"Why can't she see through this guy instead of getting upset with us?" Griffin asked his other sisters.

"She thinks we have an irrational dislike of him." Vikki, Sadie's twin, shrugged. "She can't see past her own feelings and understand why we're so worried about her."

"You can tell me it's none of my business," Abigail said. "But what is it about this guy that troubles you so much?"

"Firstly, it is your business." Kiely smiled at her. "You and Charlize are part of the family."

"And secondly, Tate Greer is a slick, expensive-suit-wearing businessman who throws his cash around. He claims to be in imports/exports but he has no visible means of making money," Griffin said.

"We've checked him out off the record, and he has no criminal record," Pippa said. "But there's just something about him…"

"I worry that the guy is really a gang boss," Griffin confessed. "Or that he's involved in some other dirty business."

"Is that really possible?" Abigail asked. "Sadie is a CSI for the Grand Rapids PD. Wouldn't she recognize a criminal if she saw one? Particularly if she got to know him well?"

"Sadie is dazzled by him," Vikki said. "She was a late bloomer. Tate is the good-looking bad guy with his tattoos and his Harley. He's swept her off her feet and I don't think she could ever see anything bad in him."

"You know her better than any of us," Griffin said. "Has Sadie ever confided that she has any hesitations or suspicions about Tate?"

Vikki shook her head. "Not to me. The only times she talks about him are to say how much she loves him. I've met him a few more times than the rest of you. He's a charmer but I didn't like him even though I can't say why. There is one thing that strikes me as odd, though."

"What's that?" Griffin asked.

"Why does he want to marry Sadie?" Vikki shrugged. "I mean, we all love her and think she's gorgeous. But I do wonder what a guy like Tate would see in our good-girl sister."

They were quietly pondering the question when Riley returned. "She's calmed down, but she wants to go home." He rubbed a hand along his jawline. "We need to be careful. We can't let our dislike of Tate cause a rift between us an Sadie."

"That won't happen." Griffin's voice was firm. "We won't let it."

"Even so, we should try to lighten up and look like we are accepting him into the family—" Riley held up a hand. "I know. I know. I feel the same way as the rest of you. At the same time, we can keep investigating him without letting Sadie know what we're doing."

"We could find out that Tate is just an obnoxious guy but that there is no harm in him," Pippa said.

"If that's the case, we'll have to welcome him into the family for Sadie's sake." Griffin's gloomy expression was reflected around the table.

"That won't happen," Riley assured him. "Our instincts will be proved right. He's a bad guy and it's just a matter of time before we find out what that means."

"Meanwhile, we have to wait for him to hurt our sister." Glumly, Kiely speared a carrot and glared at it as though she hated it.

"If he does that, he'll regret it." Griffin's words were greeted by nods from his siblings. "Now, can we forget Tate Greer while we finish this delicious meal?"

Abigail was sure that the improvement in her physical health had a lot to do with her emotional well-being. She was happier now than she'd ever been. Not even the threat of Jenna lurking in the background could destroy her newfound joy. Over the following few days, as she basked in the knowledge that Griffin loved her, she grew stronger. At the same time, her worries about getting Maya's adoption back on track remained. Until Jenna was caught, and the true story came out, Abigail's status as a mom was still in doubt.

When the nurse came for her visit, she nodded approvingly. "This wound is healing really well."

"When can I stop wearing the sling?" Abigail asked. It felt like a big step on the road to recovery. Having two arms again instead of one would make a huge difference, especially when it came to caring for Maya.

"You can take it off for short periods each day," the nurse said. "But if your arm aches, or feels tired, you must start to wear it again. I'll speak to Dr. Reynolds and ask her to arrange your physiotherapy."

"Thank you."

After walking the nurse to the door, Abigail went in search of Griffin. She found him drinking coffee in the kitchen with Emmanuel Iglesias.

"Where's Maya?" she asked.

"Sleeping." He jerked a thumb in the direction of the baby monitor. "She finished her lunch while you were with the nurse, then got a bit cranky, so I took her for a nap."

"Oh, that's good." She smiled. "Dealing with a tired baby when I only have one working arm. Well, it's something I'd rather not do."

"Emmanuel is here to give us an update about Jenna," Griffin said.

Abigail turned hopefully to the detective. "Really?"

He held up a hand. "Please don't get your hopes up. I came to see you because I thought you deserved to know where the investigation was. But that doesn't mean I have anything new to tell you."

Abigail's shoulders slumped. "So you still have no idea where she is?"

"I'm sorry," Emmanuel said. "I do have some news for you. I put out an alert to all medical facilities in the Grand Rapids area to inform me if a woman sought help for an animal bite to the left wrist. Two days ago, a woman matching Jenna's description attended a private clinic and asked for antibiotics because of an infected injury. The doctor who attended her believed the wound could have been caused by an animal bite. When we showed him pictures, he identified his patient as Jenna Avery."

"Where was this clinic?" Griffin asked.

"In the Roosevelt Park area but the address she gave was a false one."

"Of course it was." Abigail rolled her eyes.

"We've concentrated our search in that general location and the clinic visit tells us two things. One is that Jenna is still in the Grand Rapids area. The second is that she is badly injured. The doctor said the wound was deep and the infection was serious. He told her to come back and see him the following day because she might need hospitalization. She didn't return."

"Do either of those things bring you closer to catching her?" Abigail asked. She knew there was a sharp note in her voice. She also knew the police were doing their best. But their best wasn't good enough right now. She wouldn't feel safe until Jenna was behind bars and that wasn't happening.

"I know it may not look like we're making any

progress," Emmanuel said. "But we are doing everything we can to find her. And the injury that your ferret inflicted might just be what brings her in. If she is as ill as the doctor who saw her recently believes, she won't be able to manage much longer without help."

At that precise moment, Abigail's cell pinged with an incoming message. Once again, the number wasn't in her list of contacts.

Hey. How about I shoot Griffin in the head while he's out running? I'd enjoy sharing that video on social media.

Feeling slightly nauseated, she passed her phone to Emmanuel. "Jenna seems to be managing just fine."

The detective's lips tightened as he read the message. "Have you been out running since Abigail was stabbed?" he asked Griffin.

"No. But surely that's not the point?" Griffin frowned as he read the text over Emmanuel's shoulder. "Despite your efforts, Jenna is still out there, and she is feeling confident enough to send harassing messages to Abigail."

"It's not just her confidence in sending messages that worries me. It's her willingness to put her plans into action." Abigail moved her left arm slightly, feeling the pull of her injury. "She stabbed me in a public place. I'm scared that she won't hesitate to come after me and Maya even though we are living here in Riley and Charlize's home."

"I can only stress again that you have to be vigilant and let us do our job," Emmanuel said. "We will catch her."

"But will you be in time?" Abigail asked as he gave her back her phone.

"That's the plan." Emmanuel got to his feet as he spoke.

She watched him as he and Griffin walked to the door. Those words weren't confident enough for her liking. Not when her own, and her little girl's, lives depended on them.

An hour later, Abigail picked up the baby monitor and checked the battery warning light. It seemed to be in working order.

"Is something wrong?" Griffin asked.

She returned to the sofa in the den, where they had been snuggled up together enjoying an old movie. "No."

After a few minutes, she sat up straight. "Maya has been awfully quiet. Usually we hear grunts and snuffles but there's been nothing."

He grinned at her. "Just relax and enjoy it."

"I know I should." She returned the smile. "But I think I'll go check on her."

He picked up the remote and paused the movie. "Want me to go?"

She shook her head. "I'm fine. Back in two minutes."

It was foolish she knew, but the situation with Jenna was making her nervous. Of course Maya was fine but she needed to see that for herself.

"Is everything okay?" Charlize was coming out of the kitchen as Abigail headed toward the stairs.

"Yes. I'm just going to Griffin's room to check on Maya."

"But…" Charlize looked confused. "Isn't she with you?"

A tiny slither of dread trickled down Abigail's spine like a raindrop down a windowpane. "No. Griffin put her down for a nap over an hour ago."

"Yes, but then the nurse came to get her. She said you asked her to take Maya to you."

Letting out a cry, Abigail started to run up the stairs. "Get Griffin," she called over her shoulder.

Although she already knew what to expect, her heart dropped to her feet when she saw the empty crib. Her knees buckled and she felt herself falling. Before she hit the floor, a pair of strong arms caught hold of her and pulled her upright.

"What happened?" Griffin held her against his chest. "Where's Maya?"

"I'm sorry." Charlize was in tears as she stood in the doorway. "She told me she was the nurse."

Griffin already had his cell phone in his hand and, within seconds, was telling Emmanuel what had happened.

"What did she look like?" Abigail asked Charlize.

"Small and dark. She was wearing a nurse's uniform, of course."

Abigail shook her head. "The real nurse was tall and fair. I walked her to the door when our appointment was over."

Griffin ended his call. "Emmanuel is on his way over, but he already has an alert out for Jenna and Maya. I don't understand how, if she's injured, she could have carried the baby down the stairs?"

Charlize hung her head. "She asked me to carry Maya for her. She had a bag in her left hand and she explained that she couldn't hold the baby as well. It was only when we reached the bottom of the stairs that she took Maya from me." She started to cry again. "I asked if she wanted help carrying her to your room, but she said she'd be fine. And now I think about it, I briefly held her bag as she took Maya from me and it felt like it was empty."

"That's because it was a prop to disguise the fact that her left wrist was injured," Griffin said. "It's not your fault, Charlize. You couldn't have known that it was Jenna in disguise."

"Of course it's not your fault. Jenna has been waiting to trick one of us. But how did she get in?" Abigail could feel panic bubbling up inside her and threatening to boil over. "We've been so careful to keep the house secure."

"While we're waiting for Emmanuel, let's take a look and see if we can figure out how she did it," Griffin said.

When they reached the bottom of the stairs, Riley came into the hall from the kitchen and Charlize ran to him with a cry. "Thank goodness you're home."

He looked at her tear-stained face in alarm. "What's been going on?"

Griffin quickly told him what had happened.

"Let's split up and check out the downstairs rooms." He tightly clasped Abigail's hand and they headed through to the dining room.

"I can't bear this." She clung to the front of his T-shirt, scared to let go. "What if—?"

"No." He kissed her forehead. "We are not going to do 'what if.' We'll find her and she'll be fine."

She gulped back a sob before looking around the room. "I can't see any way Jenna could have got in here."

They moved on, stepping into the next room. It was little more than a storeroom, but it had a small window.

"There." Griffin pointed. "There is a broken pane and the lock has been tampered with."

"You mean Jenna could have gotten in and out of the house anytime she wanted?" Abigail swallowed hard.

"Well, with a police presence outside, I'm guessing she used the cover of darkness most of the time." Griffin frowned as he looked around the small space. "Today, she must have been concealed in here, waiting for the perfect opportunity. It came when you were busy with the nurse, I was with Emmanuel and Riley had gone out. There was only Charlize to deal with and she tricked her by dressing as a nurse."

Abigail shuddered. "The thought of her hiding out in this house, watching us, waiting to pounce… Then taking our baby girl…"

He gripped her uninjured arm. "Stay strong. For Maya."

Although she felt sick to her stomach and light-headed, Abigail clung to those words. "For Maya."

A few moments later, they heard Emmanuel's voice. Griffin called him into the storeroom and showed him the window.

"Jenna must have approached the house from the rear." The detective studied the broken window thoughtfully. "We've had a patrol car at the front the whole time."

"Can we save the speculation about the details of *how* she got in for after we have Maya back safe?" Griffin asked. "Right now, I'd rather focus on how we're going to find them."

As he finished speaking, Abigail's cell phone pinged and, with a feeling of dread, she withdrew it from her pocket. A picture of Maya filled the screen.

"My baby," she gasped.

"Forward it to me," Emmanuel said. "I'll send it for instant analysis in case there are any clues in the background."

Another picture followed. It was of a syringe next to a bottle of RevitaYou vitamins.

"What does that mean?" Abigail turned to Griffin in confusion.

"There's a text message coming through." He held the phone so they could read it together.

Your dad put ricin in his pills. He didn't care that the people who took them were dicing with death. Some would live. Some would die. Which group will Maya be in? Guess we'll find out when I inject her with the poisonous vitamins.

Abigail gave a moan and stumbled to her knees. Griffin knelt beside her, wrapping his arms around her. Looking up at Emmanuel, his voice reflected Abigail's own anguish. "We have to find them. Now."

Chapter 16

The next few hours had a nightmarish quality to them. Abigail had retreated behind a wall of silence and she was shivering wildly as though suffering from a terrible illness. Griffin tried to comfort her and, at the same time, liaise with the police and his siblings.

Emmanuel had thrown every resource available to the GRPD into the search but, with no real leads, he was struggling to track Jenna down. Although no one said the words out loud, they all knew they were racing against time. If Jenna carried out her threat to inject Maya with RevitaYou, the consequences would be unthinkable.

The Colton siblings had raced to see what they could do to help. Riley was coordinating the CI team and his sisters had mobilized everyone they knew into a task force. As a result, dozens of people were out on the road, trying to trace where Jenna could have gone after she snatched Maya. Like the police, they were finding it hard to come up with any leads.

"I'll make coffee," Griffin said. "Strong and black with plenty of sugar. Isn't that meant to be good for shock?"

Abigail didn't answer. Instead, she continued to stare at the blank screen of her cell phone as though willing something to appear on it.

"Come to the kitchen with me." He took her hand and she rose from the sofa, allowing him to lead her. Her movements reminded him of a rag doll, as though her body had no muscle or bone, nothing to give it strength or resistance.

While he prepared the drinks, Griffin kept talking, watching Abigail as he did. It would destroy them both if anything happened to Maya, but she was already crumbling. When her cell phone indicated that there was an incoming message, she almost went into orbit.

"It's her again."

He rushed to her side in time to see another picture of Maya. This time the baby was lying on a table with brightly colored cartoon characters painted on its surface. The bottle of RevitaYou and the syringe had been placed next to her.

It's almost time. Are you ready for the video?

Abigail gave a hoarse cry and covered her mouth with her right hand. She gestured wildly at her phone, but no sound came out of her mouth.

"It'll be okay—"

"No." Finally, she managed to speak. She gripped his arm so tightly that he winced. "That picture... I know where she is."

"What?"

"The table." She pointed to the image on the screen of her cell. "It's in the laboratory at Danvers University where Jenna and our colleagues worked on the miscarriage project. It's like a baby changing table, but there was a mobile above it to distract the infants when we needed to take blood, or do other tests. If you look closely, you can even see a corner of the university logo in the background."

Griffin already had his own cell phone in his hand. Emmanuel answered immediately. "Jenna is at Danvers University in one of the laboratories. Abigail will be able to guide you to the exact location. We'll meet you there."

"There's still a patrol car at your gate. They'll give you an escort."

Griffin called out to Riley. Partly to let him know what was happening, but also because he needed to get his licensed weapon from the gun safe. Minutes later, they were dashing toward the door. Then they were outside in the warm night air and running toward the car.

"Will we be in time?" Abigail asked as Griffin gunned the engine.

"We have to be."

Secure in the knowledge that he had a police car just behind him, he drove at speed through the familiar streets. It wasn't enough. If his vehicle had been powered by rocket fuel, he'd have wanted more. His daughter needed him.

When they reached the Danvers University entrance, a uniformed cop halted them. "Detective Iglesias is expecting you. He asked that you turn off your lights, then drive to the far side of the parking lot."

Griffin followed his instruction. In the darkened corner of the lot, Emmanuel was waiting for them with a number of other police officers. There was also an ambulance and a couple of paramedics standing by. Griffin and Abigail alighted from the car and Emmanuel beckoned for them to join him under the cover of a group of trees.

"I don't want to alert Jenna to our presence." He held up an electronic tablet. "I have a plan here of this part of the building. Can you show me which room Jenna is in?"

Abigail stepped forward, consulting the plan on the screen. "She's in this laboratory." She pointed to a room. "It's on the first floor and on the opposite side of the building to where we are now."

"You're basing this on a table that was in the picture she sent you. Are you certain she couldn't have moved it to another room?"

"No." Abigail shook her head firmly. "It's fixed to the wall."

"Okay." Emmanuel addressed the officers around him. "The danger in this situation is that if the kidnapper becomes aware that we are here, she may harm the baby. Therefore, I need a circle around the building, with every exit covered. But, when I decide the time is right, I will go in there alone." He looked directly at Griffin. "Is that clear?"

Griffin nodded. "Crystal."

When Emmanuel turned away to give instructions to his officers, Griffin leaned closer to Abigail. "It may be clear, but it's not happening."

After a few minutes, Emmanuel gave the order for his officers to get into position. Once they'd formed a circle around the laboratory block, he went to the front entrance. He had called ahead and arranged for the building supervisor to meet him there and disarm the security system and unlock the doors. Having removed his weapon from its shoulder holster, he stepped inside the lobby.

Once Emmanuel had disappeared from view, Griffin took Abigail's hand. "He's going to take this too slow. Is there another entrance?"

She nodded. "There's a door close to the laboratory where Jenna is holding Maya. Unless the code has been changed since I left, I should be able to get us in there." She cast a quick glance around. "I want to get Maya out as much as you do, but are you sure we shouldn't leave it to Emmanuel?"

"I'm not going to interfere with the police operation unless I have to, but he's going to play by the rules and Jenna won't. I just want to make sure we're there for Maya when things get messy."

She nodded. "Let's go."

Avoiding the police line, she led him to a smaller

entrance on the opposite side of the building. Typing the familiar code into the keypad at the side of the door, she held her breath, half expecting it not to work. Instead, there was a click, and she pushed the door open.

How many times had she entered the building this way, coffee in hand, ready to start a day's work? Now she was here to save Maya's life.

"We need to be careful," Griffin whispered as they stepped inside. "We don't want to meet Emmanuel coming in the opposite direction. He could shoot first and ask questions later."

"The laboratory is two doors down on the right."

"Here's the plan. You grab Maya while I tackle Jenna."

She nodded. "Simple but effective."

With Griffin in the lead, they slowly inched their way along the wall. Although she tried to force herself to stay positive, she couldn't help wondering why Maya wasn't crying. It was hours since the baby had last eaten or had a bottle of formula. She would be confused and missing Abigail and Griffin. Maya was going through a phase in which she was wary of strangers unless she was in her mom's arms. And Abigail couldn't imagine that Jenna had treated her gently. A baby who could scream the place down at the sight of a diaper should not be silent in these circumstances.

Griffin stopped outside the second door and raised his eyebrows. Abigail nodded. This was it. Their baby girl was on the other side.

She has to be okay...

After pausing to listen carefully, Griffin placed his hand on the door handle and slowly turned it. Abigail's hands shook at her sides, her injured arm ached from being out of the sling for so long, and she jammed her right fist against her lips to mask her noisy, ragged breathing. Her eyes were open so wide that the muscles felt strained, and as the door swung open, she followed Griffin on legs that felt stiff and clumsy.

The room was almost completely dark, the only light coming from a small desk lamp. Maya was still strapped to the table, as she had been in the picture. She was asleep. Or drugged? *Not worse. Please, not worse...*

Jenna was slumped in a chair at her side, from the way her head had dropped forward and her mouth gaped open, she appeared to be sleeping.

As soon as she saw her baby, Abigail gave a soft whimper and made a movement to brush past Griffin to get to her. He reached out an arm to hold her back, pointing to Jenna's hand. In it, she was holding the syringe that had been in the picture she'd sent.

He moved up close, pressing his lips to Abigail's ear. "Startle her and she could use it."

The tight cramps in Abigail's stomach loosened a little. From where they were standing, they couldn't see whether the syringe was empty or full. It was possible that Jenna *hadn't* already injected Maya with the RevitaYou. Griffin was right. If their girl had a chance, they had to take care.

Griffin signaled for her to move with him across the room. If they could get to the other side without disturbing Jenna, they would be able to approach her from behind. It was a long shot but all they had. Even though ice water seemed to be flowing through her veins and trickling down her spine, Abigail felt curiously calm. They were doing something. Back at the CI headquarters, when everyone else was out searching and she'd been waiting for news, she'd seriously believed her mind might just cave under the pressure.

Now, she and Griffin had taken charge. She was almost in touching distance of her baby girl...

"What?" Jenna grunted and sat up. She appeared dazed as she looked around her.

"Now." Griffin dived forward, toppling her from her chair. Jenna let out a screech of anger and sprang up, clawing at him.

Although she was concerned about Griffin, Abigail had one priority: Maya. Struggling to see in the gloomy light, she grappled with the restraints on the table. As she did, she was relieved to note that Maya was breathing, although she was definitely sleeping too soundly. She'd been drugged. But was it the RevitaYou, or had Jenna given her a sedative?

Finally, she managed to get the straps that were holding Maya in place free. Clutching her baby to her chest, Abigail stepped to one side. She needed to get Maya outside to the paramedics, but Jenna was between her and the door. She switched on the overhead light, anxiously watching what was going on and waiting for a chance to make a run for it.

Jenna was no match for Griffin's size and strength, but she had reached the desk and was hurling everything she could find in his direction. He ducked the flying objects and continued to approach her. When she picked up a pair of scissors, he paused.

"The police are outside, Jenna. It's all over."

Even though Jenna had been on the run and the bite Lucy had given her was infected, the other woman's appearance shocked Abigail. Her skin was deathly pale with brilliant crimson blotches and her eyes were red rimmed. She looked like an extra from a horror movie.

"Over for who?" Throwing the scissors at him, she dived to the floor, snatching up the discarded syringe.

As she rolled toward Griffin, Abigail cried out a warning. At the same time, Emmanuel burst into the room. As Jenna prepared to jab the needle into Griffin's leg, Emmanuel grabbed her and pinned her down. She gave a wail of mingled pain and fury as the action caused her to release the plunger and inject herself in the side.

"This stuff is poisonous. I could die."

She was still screaming as Emmanuel handcuffed her and explained that she was under arrest.

"Don't you see what this means?" Abigail turned to Griffin. "She didn't inject Maya with the Revita-You."

"Not because I wouldn't have." Jenna spat the word out. "I just wanted to torture you a little longer. All I gave her was the oral sedation we use for babies who need an MRI scan."

As she spoke, Maya hiccupped and opened her eyes.

"Let's get her checked over by the paramedics," Griffin said.

A few minutes later, they were seated in the back of the ambulance. Maya was drinking water from a sippy cup and playing with a stethoscope.

"Her vital signs are all fine," the paramedic told them. "There can be side effects from oral sedation, but they are minor. Tiredness, irritability, possibly vomiting. If you have any concerns, just call us."

"She's okay." Abigail rested her head on Griffin's shoulder. "We're all okay."

"What part of 'I'm going in there alone' didn't you understand?" Emmanuel joined them in the ambulance.

"She's our baby," Griffin said.

"I guess I'd have done the same in the circumstances." The detective sighed. "If Maya is ready to go home, we're going to need this ambulance. Jenna is screaming about police brutality and forcible ricin poisoning."

"We were there," Griffin said. "We saw what happened."

"Thanks." Emmanuel patted Maya's cheek. "Totally worth it to get this little one back unharmed."

When he'd gone, Griffin lifted Maya into the crook of one arm and placed the other around Abigail's shoulder. "Let's go and let the rest of the family know we're safe."

The whole family had gathered around the dining table to briefly celebrate Maya's homecoming. The baby, who had shown no ill effects following her ordeal, had been delighted to see everyone. Having entertained them with her whole repertoire of clapping, waving and peekaboo, she had finally fallen asleep in Abigail's arms.

Now it was close to midnight and Abigail was still watching over her as she slumbered.

"She's fine and you need to get some sleep." Gently, Griffin steered her away from the side of the baby's crib.

"I know. It's just, after everything that's happened, I almost can't believe we can stop looking over our shoulders at last."

"Why don't we take the baby monitor downstairs. I'll make us a hot drink and we can talk without disturbing Maya," Griffin said.

"I'm not sure…" She gave the monitor a wary look and he knew she was thinking of what had happened the last time they'd left Maya alone. Although her caution was understandable, he was determined to help her overcome it.

"Riley has put new locks on all the first-floor windows and I'll check on Maya regularly." He took her hand. "But Jenna is behind bars."

She nodded. "I know that. I just keep thinking about how close we came to losing her."

"And now we have her back." He led her to the door. "And she's not going anywhere ever again."

They went into the kitchen and, even though the night was warm, Griffin made hot chocolate. Once they were in Abigail's room, they switched on the bedside lamps and sat side by side on the bed.

"This is nice." She rested her head on his shoulder with a contended sigh. "Like something normal people do."

"We could go home tomorrow." He paused for a few seconds. "If you want."

"Oh." She reached across him for her drink and took a sip. "Whose home?"

"That's up to you."

She returned her drink to the bedside table before shifting position to look at his face. "What does that mean?"

"It means I'm asking you—very clumsily—if we can get married and adopt Maya together as husband and wife."

Her beaming smile was the only answer he needed. "I would love to marry you, Griffin."

"I was so scared of love that I never gave myself a chance to try it. I loved my mom with all my heart and when she died my world fell apart. I felt like nothing could be worth that same gut-wrenching pain all over again." He wrapped his arms around her, taking care not to hurt her injured arm. "But, at the same time, I craved love. I was terrified that I would drive other people away with my longing for acceptance. I can see now that was why I backed off from my Colton family. I wanted to be part of the group, but I was scared of losing them. When it came to dating, I would take a few steps, then back off, afraid of getting in too deep or coming on too strong."

She touched his cheek. "I'm so sorry you were scared."

"But that's just it. Because of you, I'm not scared anymore. I fell in love with you during the worst possible time in our lives. Your world had been shaken upside down and I wanted to be the one you could lean on to get through it. I fell in love with you in the darkest most painful days we'd both experienced. But loving you is worth it. Loving you makes me feel alive. And I know now that I deserve to know what it feels like to fall in love. Even better, I deserve to be loved."

"You do." Abigail placed a hand on his face. "And I'm looking forward to spending my whole life loving you. For me, it was a different kind of fear. I knew what happened when you love the wrong person," Abigail said. "I saw my own mom give her heart over and over and get it broken every time. And somehow, because she'd made a commitment to my dad, she was supposed to glue the pieces back together, pin a smile on her face and carry on. I knew from a very early age that I wasn't going to let that happen to me. I would never let someone else be careless with my heart."

She felt the tears on her cheeks and brushed them away. "But I know I can trust you with my heart, Griffin, just as I trusted you with our baby's life. I'm so glad we didn't let our fears hold us back from finding each other and from something so magical."

He drew her back into his arms, sliding into a half-lying position. "What sort of wedding shall we have?"

"One where Maya can be a flower girl." She answered promptly. "And, if Maya is walking, she can hold Lucy's leash as they walk down the aisle."

"Have you already planned this?"

"I might have given it some thought." She tilted her chin and gave him a mischievous smile. "There's something else I've been thinking about."

He studied her face in fascination. "What's that?"

"Remember that shower we said we'd share...?"

Chapter 17

The next day, Emmanuel came to see them. "Jenna hasn't confessed. Not exactly. But there is so much evidence against her that it doesn't really matter."

"Why did she kill Evan?" Abigail asked.

"Because he was going to fire her. She believed it was over her online adoption scam," Emmanuel said. "When Jenna was working on the miscarriage project, she'd seen an opportunity to make money and had developed the MorningStar baby con. It had worked well for her with no real issues and she made a lot of money from it. When she found out someone was on to her about her fake company, she assumed it was you, Abigail, because she knew you were looking into adoption."

"But it was me," Griffin said. "Liam and Shelby Desmond had asked me to investigate the online scam."

"And the reason why Evan had decided to let her go had nothing to do with her dirty tricks," Emmanuel said. "When we went through his computer, we found her dismissal letter in his files. Jenna was a shoddy worker and she'd been falsifying scientific evidence as part of her research. Dr. Hardin had warned her in the past, although it seems he'd given her chances because of their brief affair. This time he wasn't prepared to give her another chance."

"She killed him for that?" Abigail asked.

"People kill for less," Emmanuel said.

"But she went back and planted the bracelet at the scene," Griffin pointed out. "Are you sure it wasn't her intention to frame Abigail all along?"

"That's a possibility, I guess, but we'll never know the answer. Any half-decent defense lawyer will go for the spur of the moment scenario. Killing her boss in anger because she was devastated at the thought of losing her job sounds better than bashing his head in to frame a coworker she hated."

"But I lost the bracelet six months ago, long before the RevitaYou story broke, or before Griffin started looking into MorningStar." Abigail was confused. "Jenna and I were friends back then. If she picked up my bracelet when I lost it, why didn't she just return it?"

"Jenna's diary will be part of the evidence against her at the trial. It even gives details of how she planted the idea with Ryan Thorne of how you should 'get what was coming to you.' If you're feeling strong enough, I suggest you come and see me and read it before then," Emmanuel said. "But the answer is simple. She was jealous of you. Personally, and professionally, you were everything she wanted to be."

"So she made up the story about taking RevitaYou in order to publicly humiliate me?"

"It was a clumsy attempt. If she'd been serious, she could at least have researched what the pills looked like." Emmanuel smiled. "But I'm glad she didn't. Even though that damn green bottle gives me nightmares, Griffin was able to use it to trick her and spook her into the open."

"Yeah." Abigail rolled her eyes in Griffin's direction as she rubbed her left arm. "Thanks for that."

"Things could have gotten a lot worse," Emmanuel reminded her.

"I know." She leaned against Griffin. "I have a strange way of showing gratitude."

He smiled down at her. "But I like you anyway." He looked back at Emmanuel. "Returning to the serious conversation, do you know where Jenna was hiding out while she was on the run?"

"She was in the basement of an old house down the road."

Abigail gasped. "You thought she was in Roosevelt Park."

Emmanuel looked embarrassed. "I reached that conclusion because she sought medical help at a clinic in the Roosevelt Park area."

"So she was right here, watching us, the whole time?" Abigail shivered. "That's creepy."

"It seems she was reconnoitering the house, studying the entrances and exits, and watching who was coming in and out. We found pictures on her cell phone of the doors and windows, including close-ups of the window she smashed to get in here on the day she abducted Maya."

Abigail had to ask the next question, even though she dreaded the answer. "And the contents of the syringe?"

"Crushed RevitaYou pills mixed with water." Emmanuel grimaced. "Jenna was planning to film herself as she injected Maya with the compound and send the video to you in real time. She was slowed down by her infected wrist and took a nap. You can thank your little ferret buddy that she wasn't feeling strong enough to put her plan into action sooner."

Overtaken by a bad case of the "what-ifs?" Abigail bowed her head. Griffin placed a warm hand on the back of her neck, and, after a few seconds, she looked up again with a smile.

"I'm okay. But Lucy needs some serious treats when we get her home."

The Colton family removal machine was in full flow again. This time the team was moving furniture from Abigail's house into Griffin's apartment and taking other items to be placed in storage. They had decided that they would live at his place for the time being and make some permanent arrangements after the wedding.

"Abigail has her job back at Danvers and she's been completely cleared of all the allegations against her.

The adoption process is proceeding as planned, so it feels like life is back on track," Griffin said to Riley. He looked across at where Abigail and Charlize were sitting in the shade and sorting through a box of baby clothes. As soon as they placed anything in a neat pile, Maya, who was trying out a crawl, came over and tossed it aside. "Well, life is a whole lot better than on track. A whole lot better than before."

"And I couldn't be happier. For both of us." Riley gripped his arm.

Pippa carried a tray of lemonade out onto the lawn and everyone gathered around as if she was a rescue dog carrying brandy in a blizzard. As they took a break, Griffin checked the local news on his cell phone. One of the items caught his attention. A homicide victim had been found in Heritage Park. The man, named Robin Olver, had been shot twice at close range.

In the video accompanying the news item, the anchor reported that Olver had invested in RevitaYou, the vitamin that had been in the news lately because of its deadly ricin compound. Anyone with information was encouraged to call the tip line...

"This needs to be checked out." He sent everyone a link to the news item. "Robin Olver had eight recently broken bones."

"An even number of broken bones?" Riley looked up from his own cell phone when he'd finished reading. "You're thinking Capital X?"

"Has to be," Griffin said. "I'll call Emmanuel."

Emmanuel answered almost immediately. "Tell

me you aren't thinking of performing any more heroic acts."

"Tell me you aren't thinking of taking up a new career in comedy."

"I'm too tired to be funny." Griffin could hear background noise as though Emmanuel was in a busy office. "What can I do for you?"

"This case that's being reported on the local news channel. The homicide victim who was found in Heritage Park? He was clearly killed by Capital X."

"What leads you to that conclusion?" Emmanuel asked.

"Aside from the fact that he'd invested in RevitaYou? The guy had eight recently broken bones. You know the Capital X goons break two at a time when their borrowers can't pay up. This Robin Olver must have been one of their victims."

"You could be right," Emmanuel conceded. "It's an angle we need to look at."

Griffin looked over his shoulder at the family group on the lawn. He took a few more steps away, making doubly sure he couldn't be overheard. "My sister, Pippa, is determined to infiltrate Capital X."

"You need to talk her out of that plan. Those guys are loan sharks and they're dangerous."

"We're doing our best to change her mind, but she's pretty stubborn. If she goes ahead with it, can I count on you to take care of her?"

"Griffin, if you sister manages to go undercover and get inside Capital X, you can rest assured that I will be watching her like a hawk."

Griffin thanked him and ended the call. A hand landed on his shoulder and he turned to find Pippa studying his face. "Who were you talking to so seriously?"

He considered the matter and decided it wouldn't hurt to tell her. "Emmanuel Iglesias."

She pulled a face. "Oh. Him."

It wasn't exactly promising. "Yes. I told him about your plans to infiltrate Capital X."

Pippa sucked in a breath. "It's got nothing to do with him."

"Maybe not. But he said he'd look out for you if you go ahead with that strategy."

"That's big of him." Pippa's whole body bristled. "But you can tell Detective Iglesias that the only way I'll work with the enemy will be over my dead body." She flounced away to join the rest of the group.

Bewildered by her reaction, he went to sit on the grass with Abigail and Maya. "Why would Pippa think of Emmanuel as the enemy?" he wondered.

Abigail shrugged. "I'm sure she has her reasons. And we should probably stay out of them."

"Wise words." He grinned. "Hey. You're all moved in."

She nudged his arm. "No getting rid of us now."

Griffin slid one arm around Abigail and the other around Maya. "That's exactly the way I want it."

* * * * *

Don't miss the first installment in the
Colton 911: Grand Rapids series:

Colton 911: Family Defender *by Tara Taylor Quinn*

Available now from Harlequin Romantic Suspense
And look out for Book 3

Colton 911: Detective on Call *by Regan Black*

Available in September 2020!

WE HOPE YOU ENJOYED
THIS BOOK FROM

◆ HARLEQUIN

ROMANTIC
SUSPENSE

Danger. Passion. Drama.

These heart-racing page-turners will keep you guessing to the very end. Experience the thrill of unexpected plot twists and irresistible chemistry.

4 NEW BOOKS AVAILABLE EVERY MONTH!

COMING NEXT MONTH FROM

⬦ HARLEQUIN

ROMANTIC SUSPENSE.

Available September 1, 2020

#2103 COLTON 911: DETECTIVE ON CALL

Colton 911: Grand Rapids • by Regan Black

Attorney Pippa Colton is determined to overturn a wrongful conviction but must find a way to get the truth out of the star witness: Emmanuel Iglesias. The sexy detective is sure the case was by the book. When Pippa starts receiving threats, her theory begins to look much more convincing, if they can unearth evidence before the true killer stops them in their tracks.

#2104 COLTON'S SECRET HISTORY

The Coltons of Kansas • by Jennifer D. Bokal

When Bridgette Colton's job with the Kansas State Department of Health sends her to her hometown to investigate a cluster of cancer cases, she uncovers long-hidden family secrets that lead her back to her first love, Luke Walker.

#2105 CAVANAUGH IN PLAIN SIGHT

Cavanaugh Justice • by Marie Ferrarella

A feisty reporter has always believed in following her moral compass, but this time that same compass just might make her a target—unless Morgan Cavanaugh can protect her. Her work gets her in trouble and anyone could want to silence her—permanently.

#2106 HER P.I. PROTECTOR

Cold Case Detectives • by Jennifer Morey

Detective Julien LaCroix meets Skylar Chelsey, the daughter of a wealthy rancher, just when she needs him the most: after she stumbles upon a murder scene. Now they fight instant attraction and a relentless killer, who will stop at nothing to silence the only living witness.

YOU CAN FIND MORE INFORMATION ON UPCOMING HARLEQUIN TITLES, FREE EXCERPTS AND MORE AT HARLEQUIN.COM.

HRSCNM0820

Detective Julien LaCroix meets Skylar Chelsey, the daughter of a wealthy rancher, just when she needs him the most: after she stumbles upon a murder scene. Now they fight instant attraction and a relentless killer, who will stop at nothing to silence the only living witness.

Read on for a sneak preview of
Her P.I. Protector,
the next book in Jennifer Morey's
Cold Case Detectives miniseries.

Great. She'd get to endure another visit with the dubious sheriff. Except now he'd be hard-pressed to doubt her claims. Clearly she must have seen something to make the hole digger feel he needed to close loose ends.

Julien ended the call. "While we wait for the sheriff, why don't you go get dressed and pack some things? You should stay with me until we find out who tried to kill you."

He had a good point, but the notion of staying with him gave her a burst of heat. Conscious of wearing only a robe, she tightened the belt.

"I can stay with my parents," she said. "They can make sure I'm safe." Her father would probably install a robust security system complete with guards.

"You might put others in danger if you do that."

Her parents, Corbin and countless staff members might be in the line of fire if the gunman returned for another attempt.

"Then I'll beef up security here. I can't stay away from the ranch for long."

"All right, then let me help you."

"Okay." She could agree to that.

"Don't worry, I don't mix my work with pleasure," he said with a grin, giving her body a sweeping look.

"Good, then I don't have to worry about trading one danger for another." She smiled back and left him standing there, uncertainty flattening his mouth.

Don't miss
Her P.I. Protector *by Jennifer Morey,*
available September 2020 wherever
Harlequin Romantic Suspense
books and ebooks are sold.

Harlequin.com

HRSEXP0820

Get 4 FREE REWARDS!

We'll send you 2 FREE Books plus 2 FREE Mystery Gifts.

Harlequin Romantic Suspense books are heart-racing page-turners with unexpected plot twists and irresistible chemistry that will keep you guessing to the very end.

FREE
Value Over
$20

YES! Please send me 2 FREE Harlequin Romantic Suspense novels and my 2 FREE gifts (gifts are worth about $10 retail). After receiving them, if I don't wish to receive any more books, I can return the shipping statement marked "cancel." If I don't cancel, I will receive 4 brand-new novels every month and be billed just $4.99 per book in the U.S. or $5.74 per book in Canada. That's a savings of at least 13% off the cover price! It's quite a bargain! Shipping and handling is just 50¢ per book in the U.S. and $1.25 per book in Canada.* I understand that accepting the 2 free books and gifts places me under no obligation to buy anything. I can always return a shipment and cancel at any time. The free books and gifts are mine to keep no matter what I decide.

240/340 HDN GNMZ

Name (please print)

Address   Apt. #

City   State/Province   Zip/Postal Code

Email: Please check this box ☐ if you would like to receive newsletters and promotional emails from Harlequin Enterprises ULC and its affiliates. You can unsubscribe anytime.

Mail to the **Reader Service:**
IN U.S.A.: P.O. Box 1341, Buffalo, NY 14240-8531
IN CANADA: P.O. Box 603, Fort Erie, Ontario L2A 5X3

Want to try 2 free books from another series! Call 1-800-873-8635 or visit www.ReaderService.com.

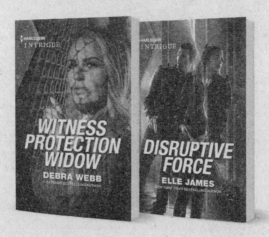

HARLEQUIN

*Heartfelt or suspenseful,
inspiring or passionate, Harlequin
has your happily-ever-after.*

With new books published
every month, you are sure to find the
satisfying escape you know you deserve.

SIGN UP FOR THE
HARLEQUIN NEWSLETTER
Be the first to hear about great new
reads and exciting offers!

Harlequin.com/newsletters

Love Harlequin romance?

DISCOVER.

Be the first to find out about promotions,
news and exclusive content!

Facebook.com/HarlequinBooks

Twitter.com/HarlequinBooks

Instagram.com/HarlequinBooks

Pinterest.com/HarlequinBooks

ReaderService.com

EXPLORE.

Sign up for the Harlequin e-newsletter and
download a free book from any series at
TryHarlequin.com

CONNECT.

Join our Harlequin community to
share your thoughts and connect
with other romance readers!
Facebook.com/groups/HarlequinConnection